"Run, Bet[h]

Arthur was alr[...] his barking a ferocious wall between her and the incoming threat.

The attacker launched a blow.

Jack danced to the side as the lead pipe whistled by his shoulder.

This attacker was targeting him, clearly. Why?

Jack shot a look behind him. Beth was still there, dialing her phone. Why couldn't she run away and do that from a safer distance? The dog continued to bark at full volume, doing his job.

The stranger's fingers gripped the lead pipe tighter. "Mind your business and stay out of things that don't concern you. Go home while you still can."

Jack seized the moment and darted forward, sweeping his foot out to snare his opponent's ankles. It would have been the perfect plan, except the dry grass concealed a deep rut that he hadn't counted on. He stumbled, his balance thrown off.

The masked man took full advantage.

Jack was able to turn his head slightly to the side as the pipe cracked down on his skull.

Pain exploded through his body with such force it paralyzed him.

As the ground rushed to meet him, the last thing he saw was Beth Wolfe, shock and fear alive in her azure eyes.

Dana Mentink is a *USA TODAY, Publishers Weekly* and nationally bestselling author. She has been honored to win two Carol Awards, a HOLT Medallion and a Reviewers' Choice Award. She's authored more than fifty novels to date for Love Inspired Suspense and Harlequin Heartwarming. Dana loves feedback from her readers. Contact her at www.danamentink.com.

Visit the Author Profile page at LoveInspired.com for more titles.

SCENT OF SABOTAGE

DANA MENTINK

LOVE INSPIRED SUSPENSE
INSPIRATIONAL ROMANCE

MIX
Paper | Supporting
responsible forestry
FSC® C021394
www.fsc.org

LOVE INSPIRED® SUSPENSE
INSPIRATIONAL ROMANCE

ISBN-13: 978-1-335-95746-7

PLEASE RECYCLE
THIS PRODUCT IS RECYCLABLE

Recycling programs
for this product may
not exist in your area.

Scent of Sabotage

Love Inspired
22 Adelaide St. West, 41st Floor
Toronto, Ontario M5H 4E3, Canada
www.LoveInspired.com

HarperCollins Publishers
Macken House, 39/40 Mayor Street Upper,
Dublin 1, D01 C9W8, Ireland
www.HarperCollins.com

Printed in Lithuania

Blessed be the God and Father
of our Lord Jesus Christ, who hath blessed us with
all spiritual blessings in heavenly places in Christ:
According as he hath chosen us in him before the
foundation of the world, that we should be holy
and without blame before him in love: Having
predestinated us unto the adoption of children
by Jesus Christ to himself, according to the
good pleasure of his will, To the praise of the
glory of his grace, wherein he hath made us
accepted in the beloved.
—*Ephesians* 1:3-6

To our amazing small group family.
Thank you for being with us on the journey.

ONE

Beth Wolfe gripped her phone, staring at the email she couldn't process. Her mind buzzed, heedless of the milling people patiently waiting their turn to meet the canine stars of Security Hounds Detective Agency. Four of the irresistible bloodhounds sported their Search and Rescue vests while they greeted the crowd. Their handlers, four of her five children, schmoozed with visitors at the community event grandly named the January Jubilee. Except for Chase, her eldest. He was charming, when called upon, but he wasn't a schmoozer.

It was an idyllic scene. The Northern California winter sun gilded the granite peaks around the normally quiet valley, a perfect backdrop for the Jubilee. The twisting pines crowded the winding road that led guests up to the event. Locals and visitors enjoyed cocoa dispensed by the local church intent on funding a mission trip for their youth. The community band in matching sweatshirts sat clustered under the gazebo, playing show tunes that set people to whistling. There was even a food truck dispensing steaming baked potatoes and chili and another offering up falafels. The town of Whisper Valley had the bases covered when they planned their festival. Nothing but good vibes all around.

But everything faded away behind the message sent to

her work email not ten minutes prior from a man she hadn't seen in more than thirty years.

Meet me a.s.a.p. It's important. I'll stay here as long as I can, followed by a location—a coffee shop at the base of the mountain—and his cell number.

Her bloodhound shoved his nose into her knee to check on her. Arthur was arthritic and slow, his muzzle glazed with silver, but he was as protective of her as her three sons and two daughters.

Why would Jack St. James be contacting her now?

Not simply a friendly check-in, not after three decades. And with such an urgent message?

Or might it be an extra dose of paranoia on her part? Certainly recent family circumstances might lead a person in that direction. The latest dangerous episode was a smuggling plot involving her eldest son, Chase, and his now fiancée, Pilar. They'd almost died and Beth's blood pressure still hadn't settled back to normal. All of her brood had faced challenges, and the stark realization that she couldn't protect them was a hard pill to swallow. Did God feel a similar frustration when His children put themselves in danger, knowingly or otherwise?

As always, she wondered for a split second about her other child, the tiny blue-eyed infant who was now a full-grown adult. The only thing she knew about him was his first name. Adam.

And the identity of his father.

Jack St. James.

Focus, Beth.

She tried to combat the nonsensical panic she felt. Everything was fine. At the moment, Steph and her husband, Vance, Roman and his wife, Emery, and their nephew Ian, and Garrett and Catherine were present and accounted for, chatting and showing off the dogs, enjoying a much deserved social time. Chase was standing in the shade, on the phone to Pilar. Only Kara and her beloved Beau were missing, taking a class in aquatic environments to help with Beau's mother's fish hatchery business.

So all was well with the Wolfes.

Her anxiety was silly. She'd ignore the message. Jack didn't have the right to command her presence. She wasn't a teenager anymore.

Arthur was staring at her, his red-rimmed eyes less acute now that he was eleven years old. A senior citizen bloodhound, but his nose, the great quivering machine that processed so much more information than she ever could, was sampling the air.

She bent to give him a caress.

Her thoughts returned to Jack St. James.

It's important.

But she couldn't leave, even if she wanted to, which she certainly didn't. She had to stay at the event, help her family clean up now that it was coming to an end and trailer the dogs back down the mountain and safely to their ranch. She'd email Jack later, with her regrets. Maybe. A sound decision, but her instincts still quivered along with Arthur's relentless nose.

Can you do something about the way you're feeling? Then do it. It was the only surefire way she'd learned to put anxiety in its place. She'd meet him. Find out what she could. Alone.

Sure, her kids would not understand her choice, but they were grown now with their own lives on which to focus. They'd babied her relentlessly after her back surgery, as if she was a paper doll, ready to rip in two at any moment. *You bless me, kids, but you don't have a clue.* It was as if they didn't remember she'd already survived a nursing career in the Air Force, the terror of seeing all of her children face life-threatening situations, the death of her beloved husband when she was only forty-four, and other circumstances her pack knew nothing about. She was stronger than they'd ever imagine. She'd had to be.

So if there was something significant underlying Jack's message, she might as well get it over with. Find out what he wanted. No one had to know.

Steph was handing out flyers for their investigation business to all the adults in the vicinity. Their sporadic search and rescue jobs were county-funded, but the private investigations cases kept the lights on.

"I'm going to head home now," she called to Steph.

Steph frowned. "Really?"

"Yes. It's winding down here. I'll meet you back at the ranch."

Garrett, her sensitive son, cocked his chin at her. "You okay, Mom?"

"Absolutely. Arthur's tired and our shift here is almost over anyway. I'll return calls and emails and get us caught up." She hurried off with Arthur before they had a moment to ask more.

As she marched toward the parking lot, she wondered if she was inventing things to worry about because she was feeling her age. At fifty-six, she was too young to sit on the sidelines, yet so much of her life was focused on her children, who didn't need her nearly as much as they pretended to. A depressing thought.

She tethered Arthur in the back and drove the steep road down the mountain, which took her a solid half hour. After that, there was nothing much between Whisper Valley and the location of the coffee shop but trees and long grass that had never found its full green after years of drought.

It took her another fifteen minutes to reach the rundown Java Jake's with its half-empty weedy parking area, bordered by a flattened sprawl of grass and a tree-lined creek bed that lost itself in the woods. She let Arthur loose.

Arthur glued his nose to the ground, following whatever scent caught his fancy.

What drew her attention was a black pickup truck. The windows were open in spite of the chill and there was someone occupying the driver's seat.

She shoved her short bob of hair behind her ears and tried not to look as if she was staring.

A flash of silver beyond the parking lot caught Arthur's attention. He flapped his ears. A vehicle tucked behind the trees? Someone making their way to their favorite fishing hole, perhaps.

The door of the truck creaked open and her stomach squeezed. A man emerged. Her nerves twanged with tension. Jack.

His tousled brown hair was messy under the brim of his baseball cap. The eyes which she knew to be a lush golden brown were hidden behind dark glasses. A five-o'clock shadow contoured his square chin.

His long-sleeve tee indicated he was muscled, solid—the fabric smooth over his trim waist—jeans slung low, ending atop his cowboy boots. He smiled and took off his sunglasses. Those eyes, sparkling and full of mischief, hadn't changed at all in spite of the crinkles around them, the lines of fatigue bracketing his mouth.

Arthur flapped his massive ears and sniffed in Jack's direction and then turned a look at her.

She fought for words, anything to cover her shock. "I... I

can't believe you're here" finally tumbled out of her mouth. What a silly thing to say. Her mortification grew.

He grinned, a double-dimpled smile. "Well, Precious, believe it, you're not dreaming me up." That sassy southern lilt. That pet name.

"Don't call me that." The words were automatic, fired like bullets at the use of a nickname she never wanted to hear again.

He cocked his head, still taking her in. "Apologies. Old habits."

Old indeed. She hadn't seen Jack St. James for more than three decades and that was best for both of them. What they'd had as young and foolish teens had ignited such pain she could still feel it reverberating deep in her bones. He came close and Arthur observed, but his attention was caught by something else, his nostrils quivering.

Jack reached down to scratch Arthur, who distractedly accepted the gesture. "You always did have a thing for dogs. Not surprised you've made a second career of it. What's his name?"

Second career. So he likely knew about her first, as an Air Force flight nurse. Did he know of her marriage then too? The death of her husband twelve years before? Her kids? He must have known where she was living, close enough to drive to this particular coffee shop to meet him. Why did it matter? She tried to regroup, give herself a mental slap to jar the senses back online. "His name's Arthur. Why did you want to see me, Jack?"

His smile dimmed and she sensed a weight in him, a gravity she hadn't seen in the younger version of the man she'd known. Her senses were still dulled. How could Jack St. James be standing right in front of her after all these years? And why?

He rested his hands on his belt. "I need to talk to you. I did some research. Saw your agency would be at the jubilee or whatever it is and I was passing through so the meeting place made logistical sense. Didn't want to interrupt or, you know, cause any awkwardness in front of your family."

Would his presence do that? *Absolutely.* Her clan was nosier than the bloodhounds. They'd want to know all about an "old friend" coming to look her up. She swallowed. "Okay. Are you here for work?" She knew he was an investigative reporter, a job he'd jumped into after his service as an army pilot. She shouldn't be in possession of that information. Shouldn't have done those sporadic Google searches a few years back.

He paused. "I'm…not sure how you're going to take this."

Casual. Just act casual. "Take what?"

He snatched off his cap and scrubbed a hand over his hair. Glimmers of silver shone at the temples now, but it was as thick as ever. Her stomach lurched as she remembered the feel of it against her fingertips, coarse and tickly.

"I'm an investigative reporter. Working on a case."

She kept her face neutral as if she hadn't known. "What does it have to do with me?"

He sighed, crammed his cap back on, stood up straight and folded his arms as he stared squarely at her. "This is kind of a big thing, the reason I came to the area. It… I mean, I had to talk to you because…"

Her throat went dry. Whatever his purpose in arranging the meeting, he was going to tell her something she definitely didn't want to hear.

She stood tall, braced her shoulders and waited.

"It's about Adam," he said and her stomach dropped to her shoes.

* * *

Her blue eyes. That hue caught somewhere between the sky and the sea. Jack thought he'd forgotten that unusual color, but it was just as familiar as it ever was, as if the decades didn't stand between them.

But he had to face up to those forgotten years. And what he'd done. She had to know.

The slight breeze ruffled her hair, white blond now, a color she could never get from a bottle. Not gray or silver, but a shining platinum. Nature's gift. The shock was written all over her face at the mention of their son's name. Not surprising, but now he was second-guessing his decision to tell her. Was it really necessary? But the milk was spilled. No turning back.

He cleared his throat. His stomach hadn't been this knotted since he'd been an embedded journalist with a unit in the Ghazni province in Afghanistan, narrowly avoiding being blown up while crossing a bridge. "I wanted to be sure you knew, before I start on this case, that…" He stopped.

Arthur growled.

The dog's attention was riveted to the trees behind them. Someone approaching? More likely a squirrel or raccoon.

He'd wait for an uninterrupted moment. Had to.

"What about Adam?" Beth said, undistracted. That was textbook Beth too. Direct. Determined. Never played games and never would.

He almost smiled, but Arthur stood on rigid legs, barking at full volume. Jack spun to see what had upset the dog.

A man rushed forward, a blocky figure wearing a ski mask. A segment of pipe was gripped in his gloved fingers.

Jack's muscles went wire taut. "Beth, get out of here."

Arthur was already in action, backing up to Beth, his

barking a ferocious wall between her and the incoming threat.

Jack faced the danger and put them both behind him. How had he led trouble straight to Beth? Why had he decided to come and talk to her? Now? There was no window for self-recrimination.

Arthur kept up the racket. Jack didn't know if the dog would bite, but he wouldn't want to test it. The attacker wasn't fazed. Clearly he wasn't there merely to intimidate.

Now they were both in a boatload of trouble. "Run, Beth," he told her. "Get clear."

He heard her move, but he wasn't sure if she was intending to stubbornly defy him and try to intervene or go and summon help. Never could tell with Beth. The attacker launched a blow.

Jack danced to the side as the lead pipe whistled by his shoulder.

His assailant regrouped and tried again. Jack stumbled, falling, landed on his stomach, quickly rolling and scrambling to his feet again. At least he was drawing the danger farther away from Beth and her dog. This attacker was targeting him, clearly. Why? Wouldn't be the first enemy he'd attracted in his line of work, but he wasn't about to let Beth or Arthur get hurt.

Jack made it to his feet, fists in front of him for all the good that would do against a metal pipe.

He shot a look behind him. Beth was still there, dialing her phone. Why couldn't she run away and do that from a safer distance? The dog continued to bark at full volume, doing his job. Jack wasn't his person to protect. *All right, Jackie boy. Take control.*

"If you think you're gonna get rid of me, you're wrong,"

Jack said. Then he flashed his most cocky "I'm the smart-est guy in the room" grin.

The stranger's fingers gripped the pipe tighter. "Mind your business and stay out of things that don't concern you. Go home while you still can."

Jack seized the moment and darted forward, sweeping his foot out to snare his opponent's ankles. It would have been the perfect plan, except the dry grass concealed a deep rut that he hadn't counted on. He stumbled, his balance thrown off.

The masked man took full advantage.

Jack was able to turn his head slightly to the side as the pipe cracked down on his skull.

Pain exploded through his body with such force it para-lyzed him.

As the ground rushed to meet him, the last thing he saw was Beth Wolfe, shock and fear alive in her azure eyes.

TWO

A second after Jack was knocked to the ground, Beth heard a vehicle slam to a halt. In a flash, Chase and his blocky canine Tank sprinted into view, followed by Garrett and Steph, their dogs galloping alongside. Soon the area was full of people and dogs, but the attacker had disappeared into the woods.

Beth pointed. "He ran there."

Chase, Steph, and dogs Chloe and Tank took off before she finished the sentence. Garrett put his dog into a sit and went immediately to her. "Mom?"

She waved him off. "Unhurt."

"We decided to pack it in early and leave Roman to finish up," he said as she dropped to her knees next to Jack. "Got off the mountain and we noticed your vehicle parked here."

That would require a later explanation on her part. Her fingers shook so hard she almost couldn't feel Jack's pulse. She thanked God when she saw the steady rise and fall of his chest. With one hand she cradled the back of his neck to stabilize his spine.

Garrett dialed the police and bobbed his chin at Jack. "Who is this, Mom? Do you know him?"

A good question after so many years. "I used to. His name is Jack St. James. He's an old college friend."

Garrett spoke into the phone and then to her. "The attacker, did he take anything? Was it a robbery?"

But she was focused on other things. Jack was alive and breathing but head injuries could be catastrophic as she fully knew. His eyelids fluttered and she leaned close, her palms still behind his neck.

"Jack? Can you hear me?"

He slitted one eye. "You okay?" he croaked.

Tears of relief stung her eyes and she blinked them away. "Yes, but you're not. Ambulance is on its way. Stay still."

He didn't. He struggled against her and then pushed away Garrett's restraining hands too.

"You could have a spinal injury. Stop moving," she commanded in her military nurse tone.

Jack continued to try to sit up. "Never could boss me, P. Not going to happen now."

Garrett jerked a look at her and tried in his own soothing way. "Mr. St. James? My name's Garrett. I'm one of Beth's sons. Help's on the way. How about you lie still, huh? You got a good crack on the head. It's best to—"

Jack sat up abruptly, immediately clutching his skull with a groan.

Beth tensed. Stubborn man could not follow the simplest directions. No wonder women lived longer.

Garrett smiled. "I guess you really *can't* boss him, Mom."

She kept hold of Jack's forearm in case he passed out. How much had her perceptive son gleaned about her former relationship with Jack? Had he caught the nickname? She felt like a nervous teenager. *Come on, Beth. You're fifty-six. Act like it.* She burned to ask Jack about Adam. Why had he brought up the son they'd given up for adoption at birth? Why now?

Chase and Steph returned with their canines.

"He made it to his vehicle and took off," Steph said, breathing hard. "A silver van. We couldn't get the plate but cops are alerted. What happened?"

She gave them the bare-bones facts as she checked the back of Jack's head for bleeding. He had a lump the size of an egg forming and he grunted when she palpated it.

Chase shoved the curly hair back from his brow. "Why would some attacker leap out of the bushes and club him if it wasn't a robbery?"

Beth kept close attention on Jack's breathing and level of consciousness. "I have no idea. Random attack?"

Chase shook his head. "I don't think so. You were meeting him here? Or you just ran into him when you stopped for coffee?"

No sense trying to fool them. "Jack emailed me. Asked me to meet him."

"And you didn't want to share that before you took off?" Chase asked.

She shrugged. "You all were busy."

"Okay," Garrett said, but she knew he wasn't convinced. "Why did you want to meet her, Mr. St. James?"

They all stared at Jack. "Call me Jack." He offered a roguish smile. "We go way back. I was in the area."

"Uh-huh. Another question. Do people beat you up on a regular basis?" Chase asked.

"No, but they probably want to," Jack said.

That got a chuckle. At least he was with it enough to crack jokes. A good sign.

The ambulance arrived along with Officer Lon Blythe, a friend of Chase's.

While the medics examined Jack, Blythe asked questions. Beth stayed close, eager to hear the answers. The first few were unenlightening.

No, Jack couldn't guess the identity or motive of the man who'd attacked him.

No, he hadn't received any threats of late.

No, he wasn't staying in Whisper Valley or nearby Copper Top.

Blythe tapped the information into his phone. "Do you have any idea why someone would want to attack you, Mr. St. James?"

Her breathing went shallow.

He shook his head slowly. "No."

"You told me you were working on a case," Beth said, deciding to omit the mention of Adam unless it became crucial. Not a topic she wanted to bring up. Ever.

He blinked. "A case?"

An uneasy feeling coalesced in her stomach. "Yes," she said. "But you were attacked before you could finish explaining. You don't remember that either?"

He was silent a moment. "No. I don't."

Did he remember mentioning their son? Her body felt as though it was on fire.

Blythe and the medic exchanged a look. "Where do you live, Mr. St. James?"

"Portland, Oregon, on a boat. I'm fifty-seven years old, no pets, no spouse or kids. See? I remember all the pertinent details."

No spouse and no kids. Her nerves twinged. Had he never found anyone to share his life with?

Blythe made notes. "Best to get you to the hospital anyway."

Jack shook his head, frown lines furrowing his brow. "I'm okay. No hospital for me."

Blythe appeared as though he'd been prepared for such a refusal. "Sir, I think that's ill-advised."

"So do I," Beth said. "And everyone else standing here agrees."

Garrett cocked his head at her strong tone. He was always much more sensitive to nuances than his twin, Steph, or the impetuous Chase. Garrett and her youngest, Kara, were like bloodhounds at sniffing out emotions. She softened her words. "Memory loss indicates you're concussed. You could have a possible brain bleed. That could be fatal."

"Nah. Head like cement." Jack waved a hand and got to his feet. "See? Not even wobbly."

"Still, though," Blythe tried. "It would be the safest choice. I can't force you to go to the hospital, but I definitely don't want to see you driving for the next twenty-four hours."

"We can give him a ride," Garrett said. "Where are you staying?"

Beth was interested in that answer. He'd mentioned he was passing through. Why look her up in person? If he had news about Adam he could have relayed it in the same email he'd used to contact her or even dial her direct phone line. That info was on the internet for anyone to see.

"A hotel," Jack said, after a pause. "I've got reservations, but I can't recall which one."

Beth's breath hitched. Memory loss was a bad indicator and a clear signal he ought to be going straight to the emergency room as any sensible person would.

Jack fumbled for his phone and brought up a screen. "Aha. Online reservation at a place in Cutter Creek."

"Cutter Creek?" Garrett frowned. "That's an hour from here in the next county. Got friends there? Family?"

Jack shook his head gingerly. "No one."

Cutter Creek was indeed a full hour away in a parched valley, a town that had struggled hard in the economic downturn. No nearby airport. No real tourist attractions save for an aging amusement park. Why would Jack be staying there?

"Got significant wildfire activity in those parts," Blythe said.

A painful five years of drought had left the entire region arid. The recent winter storm had done little more than produce dry lightning, which had ignited several fires on acres ripe for torching.

Another reason to avoid that particular area. The expression on her children's faces indicated they couldn't imagine why Jack would stay there either.

Blythe tried for another few minutes to talk Jack into a hospital visit.

Jack thanked the officer. "I'll give it a while. If I develop problems, I'll check myself in immediately, I promise."

If he lived long enough.

Jack rubbed a hand over his chin. "Is there a cab company around here I can call?"

"We can drive you, soon as we're clear here. Take your truck too," Chase said.

"I'll drive him." Beth's sudden offer surprised them all.

Chase raised a brow. "But—"

Jack started to protest, but she cut him off.

"He's a friend and you all have to get the dogs home. Garrett, can you and Chase take the trailer back? Steph and Vance, would you be willing to tag team and drive Jack's truck to the hotel before you head home?"

Steph nodded. "Yes, but I have to feed this big guy first or he'll whine all the way."

Vance shrugged. "What can I say? I have a quick metabolism. We'll fuel up here and we promised Kara we'd pick up a part for her chicken coop, then we'll drop off the truck. Okay?"

They all agreed.

"Great. Arthur and I will drive Jack then." Outwardly, an act of a good neighbor. But she had other motives. It occurred to her that Jack might not remember everything, but he could very well be hiding information as well. Or were there things he didn't want to discuss in front of a crowd?

Thinking about sitting in a car with Jack St. James ratcheted her nerves tight. She'd only grill him about the pertinent facts. There would be no room for dwelling on their wrecked past. He would explain what he knew about Adam and they'd leave the rest unspoken.

The memory flooded in before she could stop it. Nineteen-year-old Jack, handsome, eyes like melted chocolate in the lights of the hospital room that smelled of antiseptic and a raggedy bouquet of cheap carnations.

"We don't have to give him up. We'll get married. Raise him together."

Her, an eighteen-year-old college dropout, waiting tables and living on a friend's couch. She'd been so desperate for a love she'd later learned couldn't be fulfilled by any human relationship. "We can't make that work and you know it. We hurt each other. We always will. It's wrong to inflict that on a child. I want him to have a good life."

Jack's face had gone hard then, like a granite cliff, stark and exposed. "He's mine too. You don't get to make the decision for both of us."

But in the end he'd agreed, because it was the best thing. They'd named their son Adam, and let him go.

She wouldn't forget the way Jack touched a fingertip to his newborn son's perfect cheek, tears sliding down his own. The one and only time she'd seen him cry. And then the look he'd given her before he'd left. Anger, shame, blame, as if she'd betrayed him.

"You're right," he'd said, voice cracking like brittle bones. "He deserves better than you and me."

And then they'd parted ways.

She realized they'd reached her SUV. Opening the back door, she attached Arthur to his tether and made sure his blanket was spread out across the covered seat. It wasn't purely spoiling— bloodhounds exuded all manner of scents, hair, saliva and other by-products and an extra barrier was helpful. And if a blanket helped ease the arthritis pain in Arthur's hind legs, she'd make sure she always had one at the ready. This one was his favorite, a thick, fleecy fabric patterned with flamingos that he seemed to love the best. Arthur executed an awkward three-point turn before he settled onto the blanket with a sigh that fluttered his fleshy lips.

Jack grabbed an overnight bag from his truck and climbed gingerly into the passenger seat. She got behind the wheel.

"I hate being a passenger."

"Hard to be you," she said, driving them out of the lot onto the highway.

He groaned. "You have no idea."

They hadn't cleared the lot when her question bubbled out. "I want to know why you mentioned Adam."

Jack cocked his head and a new rush of anxiety twisted her insides.

"I don't remember," he said.

Jack tried to keep the pain out of his voice as the miles rolled by. It was strange, driving along in a car with Beth Wolfe, the woman he'd known as Beth Camden. She wasn't eighteen anymore, but if possible, she'd become even more attractive—the fuss-free hair that absorbed the winter sunlight, the confident way she held the wheel, the softened curves of her body.

But that was an idea best left unexplored. *You got problems, Jackie boy. How about you figure those out, huh?*

To his horror, he did not remember why he would have brought up the name of their child. It was unfathomable.

Adam. Their child was a stranger. But the fact didn't ring true. He had the sense that he knew his son. Somehow. The pounding in his skull wasn't helping him think clearly. He needed space to gather up the scattered pieces of his brain. And he needed an aspirin. Desperately.

Beth wasn't about to let the topic go. "All right. Your memory will hopefully improve, but in the meantime maybe we can figure out why you came to me. You weren't visiting to catch up. If so you would have told me you were coming, not shown up out of the blue, and you wouldn't have mentioned Adam."

"I'd like to explain it, I really would, but the old gray cells are on strike. It's a void." He blew out a breath. There was an overwhelming sense in his gut of a boulder waiting to roll downhill on top of him. Adam, his baby son, the one they'd given up. *Think, think, think.* He'd never talked to Adam—had he? But if he hadn't, why would he have told Beth they needed to discuss him?

"Is that the truth?" she snapped. "You forgot?"

"Do you know me to be a liar?" he fired back.

She flashed a look at him that kindled to anger and died away quickly. "No, but I don't really know you at all anymore."

Her response was harsh. His question had been too. He massaged his temples. "It's a long drive, Beth, and I've got a monster headache. You're not going to grill me the whole way, are you?"

She shrugged. "I'll give you a break for a little while."

He tried his best not to grimace with every bump of the wheels. "Your family seems nice."

The comment seemed to startle her into a nervous response. "Thank you. You'd like Roman too. He was adopted after my husband passed, but half the time I don't even remember that."

So she'd adopted. Interesting.

She stared at him for a moment. "You said you had… no kids?"

After a pregnant pause, he said, "No. My marriage didn't work out. I'm sorry about your husband."

"I…" she started, but the words trailed off.

The sky was hazy with smoke.

"Wildfires burning east of Cutter Creek," she said, finally.

"A threat to the town?" A van appeared behind them in the side-view mirror.

Arthur popped his head up to look.

"Not yet. They've evacuated north of there but Cutter Creek is still safe so far."

"Hmm." He watched the van drop back some. There was little traffic, so why would the other vehicle slow? He eased in his seat to try and quell the ache that reached from his skull to his boots. The van dropped back even farther, but stayed there, like some fly hovering on the edge of a tasty morsel.

Beth broke into his thoughts. "What are you looking at?"

"Nothing."

"Not nothing. What?"

He figured she wouldn't let it go. "The silver van behind us."

She peered into the rearview mirror. "Steph said the attacker escaped in a van. Following?"

"Don't know. There are tons of silver vans, but if this is the guy, I don't want you involved so—" He didn't finish his sentence before she'd flipped on her indicator.

"Let's find out," she said.

Before he could argue, she'd exited the freeway at the nearest off-ramp, sliding neatly into a gas station parking lot, engine running.

He glared at her. "What part of 'I don't want you involved' was unclear?"

She gave him that look, the one that was equal parts adorable and aggravating. "You can't boss me either, Jack."

And that was the stone-cold truth. They watched in silence as the van sailed by, the driver a vague shadow, and noted a tow hitch on the rear, nothing else at all remarkable.

Jack exhaled. "Not following." He tapped his temple. "Just my scrambled brain, I guess." He held up a palm. "And before you begin the inquisition, I'm still not going to the hospital. I will be a model patient at the hotel where I will rest quietly, drink lots of fluids, eat a full serving of veggies before I brush and floss, and tomorrow I'll drive home if I can't remember why I came here." He held up his hand to stop her comment. "It will come back to me, I'm sure, about Adam. I'll call you as soon as I remember, okay?"

"What about the case?"

He shrugged. "When I'm back at my office I'll be able to put the pieces together."

"Don't you have computer files you can access from your phone?"

He laughed. "I haven't changed, Precious. I mean, Beth," he corrected. "Still a paper-pencil guy."

"I feel like you're not telling me everything."

"We haven't seen each other in decades. You hung up during my one and only phone call, remember? There's too much to cover for both of us." He shouldn't have said it. He could practically see her flinch, her mouth forming into a hard line. There was no way to smooth it over, joke it away, so he left the remark sitting there between them, sharp and cutting like a broken pane of glass. The last thirty minutes of the drive felt endless and though he kept a sharp eye out for the silver van, it didn't reappear.

When she finally pulled up at the cramped two-story hotel with the vacancy sign blinking, she quirked a small smile. "I see you still don't give much regard to your accommodations."

He chuckled, even though it made his head pound. "I don't care where I sleep as long as there's a mattress and no roaches. I don't like bugs." But his body was voicing all kinds of complaints at the moment. Good mattress or bad, he couldn't wait to lie down because his head felt like a timpani drum, but there were a few things he had to look into before he earned some rest. He wanted to be alone before he dove in.

"You're really planning on going home tomorrow?"

"Cops said they can get anything else they need over the phone, so yes." Unless his memory suddenly returned and he recalled what was so urgent that he'd come stay in Cutter Creek.

He got out and she rolled down the passenger window.

"Jack," she started, stopped, started again. "Whatever you'd been trying to tell me before you were hurt, it was important." She pursed her lips. "I mean, if you'd look me up after all these years and mention Adam, especially when—"

"When you called me a stubborn ox during our last phone call on your twentieth birthday?"

She blushed to the roots of her hair. "Um, I'm sorry I said that."

"It's okay. It was probably true."

She looked surprised. "Well, anyway, I should have been more mature than to resort to name-calling."

"We've both done a lot of growing since then."

She took a breath. "Jack, I have a bad feeling."

"You and me both. My head is killing me." He smiled. "I know that's not what you meant. Don't worry. I'll be fine and I'll figure this out. You go on home now before it gets dark."

When she hesitated, he called a goodbye to Arthur in the back seat.

"My kids should be here soon. They'll leave your truck and drop the keys in the office so they won't disturb you," she said.

Or maybe because she didn't want them to have a chance to ask him too many questions about their past? Her scars were deep. His too.

He bent to look at her through the open SUV window and gestured for her phone.

She handed it to him and he programmed in his cell phone number before returning it.

"Beth, I don't know what I'm involved in, but I don't want it anywhere near you. I regret dragging you into this. It's a mistake I can correct. Drive straight home, okay? Don't stop anywhere. Text me when you get back."

"I—"

"It really was good to see you, by the way, in spite of everything. Take care of yourself and I promise I'll call when my brain is unscrambled."

She closed her mouth and nodded, not quite looking at him. After he watched her drive away, he checked in at the hotel and accepted his key card.

"When did I make the reservation?" he asked the clerk. The man arched a brow at him.

"I had a head injury and my past is a little foggy."

"Oh. Okay." He consulted the screen. "Reservation was made yesterday morning."

"Thanks," he said. Tuesday morning he'd made a reservation in an out-of-the-way town and contacted Beth to meet her before he made it there. What did that tell him?

The pounding in his skull would not be quieted as he trudged to the appointed room.

He eased onto the bed with a groan, his conscience pricking him. He hadn't been completely honest with Beth. It had felt necessary to keep her far away from whatever mess he'd gotten himself into, especially since someone had been watching him and knew he was connected to her. No way would he risk her safety. It was true that he was a paper-pencil guy, but even dinosaurs had to get up to speed. Particularly, reporter dinosaurs who researched online. He had computer files and he could indeed access them from his phone.

But Jack was also a suspicious man, wary of the million ways information could be hacked and stolen—a cautious practice when he was doing his job in enemy territory. He thumbed open the digital file on his phone, created three days before. It was brief, indicating he'd had only an initial conversation. The information was scant.

The initial D., and a cell phone number.

A. reports no contact from Tess.

Tess? And who was A.? Their son Adam? His heart hammered.

He pulled up his contacts and sure enough there was a number for A., no name spelled out. Since he faithfully deleted his text messages, there was no helpful information there.

Might as well dive in.

He tapped a text message.

A. It's Jack. Need to talk.

He waited, but there was no reply.

If there was a concern about the woman Tess, why wouldn't the cops get to the bottom of it? And why had Jack felt it necessary to meet with Beth about Adam? It made him think that A. might actually be their son.

His stomach growled and he remembered he hadn't eaten anything since the gas station breakfast burrito he'd snagged hours ago. He'd seen a vending machine in the lobby that took bills. That was about as far as he'd be able to travel in his current condition.

Behind the dollar bills in his wallet, he found something unfamiliar—a neatly folded, quarter-page flyer, printed out from a computer. He eased it out, mind spinning.

Meadowlands Amusement Park.

Meadowlands Amusement Park was only a few miles away, which explained why he'd come to Cutter Creek. It sure wasn't to ride roller coasters and eat cotton candy. Here was his case. Another piece falling into place.

The answers to his questions had to be at the amusement park.

And he was going to find them.

And he had no intention of filling Beth Wolfe in on his plans, because whoever had attacked him wouldn't hesitate to target her too.

If their son was involved, he'd take care of his boy like he should have been doing all these years.

Amusement park, here I come.

THREE

Beth dutifully texted Jack when she arrived back at home at the dinner hour. The trip had taken longer than anticipated when she'd had to stop to have a flat tire changed.

His reply was immediate.

All settled into luxury room 17. Still conscious. Take good care of yourself.

Ironic from a man who was ignoring all sound medical advice. A ripple of foreboding surged along her spine. Jack had secrets. And he was in trouble. What about their son? How was Adam involved?

In the kitchen of the tidy ranch-style home, she was greeted by a bunch of adults gathered around the table eating peanut butter and jelly sandwiches while the dogs scarfed kibble.

Beth greeted everyone and poured Arthur his dinner too. He stirred it with his paw before he started to eat, an odd little quirk that always made her smile.

Garrett pushed a sandwich over to his mom when she joined her kids.

"Chase's night to cook?" Beth said with a chuckle.

Chase rolled his eyes. "Everyone complained so much about my spaghetti I went with something easier."

"The spaghetti was fine—it just needed to be cooked," Steph said.

Chase shrugged. "Ha ha. Thank you for your input, Betty Crocker."

"I thought you'd beat us home, Mom," Steph said.

Beth sighed. "Tire trouble. Did you get the truck dropped off okay?"

"Sure. Left the keys in the office as you suggested." Steph was clearly puzzling over why her mother hadn't suggested she hand them to Jack personally.

Beth grabbed the pitcher of iced tea and busily refilled everyone's glass.

They ate sandwiches and discussed the inevitable topic, the attack on Jack.

"Did he remember anything else about why he came to see you?" Steph asked.

"No." Not that he was admitting to, anyway. No sense in bringing up Adam. The kids didn't need to know about that part of her life. How would she explain it? *I had a baby as a teen. I gave him up for adoption and never lifted a finger to find him? Didn't ever mention your half sibling to you all?* Only her husband, Martin, had known her secret.

"Police have nothing much to go on," Steph said. "Vance is playing basketball with some of his department contacts so he might collect some useful information, but I doubt there's much to be had."

Chase took a bite out of his second sandwich. "Glad Jack's left town if he's bringing trouble like that with him."

Steph elbowed him. "That's sensitive."

"What?" Chase chewed and swallowed. "We don't want Mom around some guy with a target on his back, do we?

How well did you know this Jack anyway, Mom?" That was Chase. Straight to the point. If he hadn't asked the question, Steph likely would have.

"Same high school graduating class?" Garrett accompanied his query with an encouraging smile. He was so like her late husband, Martin. Direct, yes, but in such a gracious way it hardly seemed like a question.

"No. Jack is a year older." She got up quickly before they could ask anything further, and poured herself a glass of water. "What's the schedule for tomorrow?"

She remained facing the kitchen window, unwilling to see if her children were exchanging curious glances at her abrupt change of subject.

"You've got the trip to Redding tomorrow, Mom. Staying over two nights, right?" Steph said, consulting the computer schedule.

"Yes. It's the regional search and rescue conference so Security Hounds should represent."

"Taking Arthur?" Garrett asked.

"Of course. I already packed for both of us yesterday." Everything they could possibly require plus supplies for a shelter donation.

Steph drummed her fingers on the table. "All right. Vance and I are coordinating a training with the East County Bloodhound Association. That's a three-day gig."

"And Kara's gone with Beau, so that leaves me and Roman to cover the shop while Garrett finishes up his case." Chase took his plate to the sink and stretched to his full six feet plus.

"Sure you can spare the time away from Pilar to answer the phones?" Roman spoke up from the end of the table. Roman was the quietest of the bunch unless he was teasing Chase about his new fiancée.

Chase grinned. "Turns out, she's pretty self-sufficient. And anyhow, if the search and rescue business stays calm, you and I can get that floor laid down in your upstairs bathroom."

Roman and his family had already moved into the new house the Wolfes had helped build on Pilar's family land, but with Emery's father and sister facing health challenges and with their young nephew to raise, elements of the project remained unfinished.

Beth yawned. "Thanks for the dinner. I'm going to take a shower and hit the sack early." Her kids would soon head to their respective homes. It was still an adjustment that Steph had moved to a nearby condo with Vance, and Roman to his newly built home. Garrett had his own place with Catherine, and Chase had taken over Roman's trailer parked on the property until his marriage to Pilar took place. Only Kara still shared the ranch home with her.

She kissed and hugged all her children, relishing yet again the beauty of the family she and Martin had made. The tiny beat of sadness tapped on her heart for the child she hadn't known, the one she'd given away that was now top of mind since Jack's arrival.

"Grateful you weren't hurt today, Mom," Garrett said. "And we're all praying for Jack."

She squeezed him close and waited for Arthur to finish eating so she could take him outside. Both of them could use some clean mountain air to clear their heads before they ended their tumultuous day.

The next morning, Beth tiptoed quietly out to her car. Steph was already up, moving about the house trying not to wake Vance. Since Beth felt groggy and out of sorts, she had simply helped herself to a travel mug of coffee, and after

Arthur's morning constitutional, she hit the road without speaking to any of her children.

In the back, Arthur snoozed happily on his flamingo blanket as she tried to make sense of the attack. Her thoughts returned to the strange events of the previous day. She felt the same surge of unease that had kept her awake the night before.

Jack had an enemy. Was it possible Adam had one too?

Adam would be in his late thirties now. What kind of a man was he? Did he resemble her? Jack? Have their same personality traits? That could be a flammable combination.

Her brain kept replaying the memory of the pipe cracking down on Jack's skull, the silver van, the sense that what Jack couldn't remember was vitally important. Why should she feel this intense worry about him? They weren't connected anymore. Hadn't been for decades.

Arthur let out a long rumbly snore. He'd be happy to see other dogs at the conference. The large group of adults wouldn't be a problem for him either. But he wouldn't settle fully, nor sleep in total serenity, until they were home again.

Neither would she. Nearing the cutoff to the freeway, she passed a crew of emergency workers, loading their wildland gear. They'd be heading to the foothills, where the fires were threatening to gobble ever more acres of California's dry grass and brush. The smoky air added to her malaise, making the familiar road strange, her direction ominous.

Engine idling, she waited for the firefighters to vanish in the distance.

She knew what she should do. Go to the conference. Forget about Jack. He'd call about Adam if he got his memory back, and if not, her life would continue on the same trajectory. Wouldn't it?

Seconds ticked into a minute. And then, with a quick turn of the wheel, she was heading for Cutter Creek.

"We'll just check," she told Arthur. "Make sure Jack's left town. If not, be certain he hasn't collapsed from a head injury." Then she'd get back on the road and arrive a few hours late, missing only the keynote speaker at the conference. "You don't mind, do you, Lovebug?"

The lovebug sighed in his sleep.

At least she didn't have to worry about him chewing a hole in the seat like Roman's dog, Wally, who was constantly trying to excavate the foam as if the inner springs were some sort of prize. The miles passed quickly and though she saw heavy columns of smoke, the fire seemed to be continuing in its path. Everyone in the rugged backlands of California knew it could all change with a single spark and a puff of capricious wind. Wildfires had consumed whole towns in their parched state, one small flame turning into a conflagration. Memories of Southern California's devastating blazes stayed fresh in everyone's minds.

Smoke aside, the drive to Cutter Creek was uneventful. Her heart beat faster as she neared the hotel parking lot. A quick scan revealed Jack's truck was not there. Had he actually left for home like he'd said? Of course. What else would he have done in a strange town where he knew no one? Then again, maybe Adam lived in Cutter Creek and Jack had forgotten. Could he be the reason Jack was in town? Was it possible her firstborn child had been living hours away from her without her knowledge?

Her nerves refused to settle.

"How about a quick walk before we head to the conference?" She parked in the hotel lot, let Arthur out and clipped on his lead. He sniffed at the forlorn clumps of crisp grass and the whiff of smoke in the air.

The curtains were drawn across the window of the room Jack texted that he'd rented but not completely.

Casually, she led Arthur along the walkway that connected the rooms. No one was around, but she tried to look as innocent as possible as she walked Arthur by. A quick glance through the open drapes showed her everything she needed to know. Jack's coat was still draped neatly over the chair, next to the desk, and a shaving kit sat on the bed. He hadn't checked out.

Not an indicator of anything untoward. He might have decided to grab some breakfast before leaving. Great idea. Wouldn't hurt to procure a second cup of coffee and a bagel to tide her over for the long trip to Redding. She explained the new plan to Arthur as they loaded up and drove into town. There was only one café along the main strip, a place with a stone facade called Snowy's. No truck, but maybe he'd parked in the rear lot.

Since there was a pet-friendly sign in the window, she walked in with Arthur. The dozen or so tables were mostly empty. None of them occupied by Jack.

So much for the theory that Jack went for a bite to eat. She took her bagel and coffee to go.

As they exited, she drew back as fast as she could. A silver van was parked in a space, idling. *The* silver van? Quickly she went back inside and guided Arthur out the back door. They hurried into the lot and made their way to the brick corner before she stopped and took a fast look. The van driver was speaking angrily on his phone. Deep voice, hairy forearms.

Arthur growled and she quieted him. Was it the man who'd attacked Jack? She couldn't see much of the occupant, so she eased a little farther forward.

"He'll get the message," said the male voice.

A pause.

"You asked me to handle it and I did. If you don't like the methods, do it yourself. I rushed back on the first plane to enact your little plan, remember."

She could get a better look if she leaned out a tiny bit more. Mistake.

His blue eyes caught her movement in the rearview mirror. He cranked the van into Reverse and sent the vehicle hurtling back toward her.

"Away," she called to Arthur as they dove toward the safety of the building. The van smashed against the brick corner, sending shards raining down before the gears ground and it took off toward the exit. She was unable to discern the license numbers on the mud-splattered plate as she ran to her car, tethered Arthur and rushed in the direction the driver had taken.

She was certain now he was Jack's attacker. She prowled the street slowly, peering into every lot and side street. As soon as she got a direction, she would call the police.

Ahead she saw a flash of silver. She goosed the gas, but there were a few cars between them.

She dropped in behind a sedan, where she could keep eyes on the van. Arthur stared out the window, tuned to her tension. She followed for several miles into a dingier part of town where many of the businesses were boarded up. The traffic was light so she had to stay back a fair distance. When a tractor pulled out onto the road from a side street, she hit the brakes. Fingers drumming, she waited impatiently. When the obstruction cleared, the van was gone.

Gone where? She idled, considering the streets the van might have taken off the main road. What was down this way?

To the left was a sharp turn that led to a storage facility but she saw no sign of the van. To the right, a series of businesses—tiling, plumbing and a tow yard. Again, her quarry had not parked anywhere she could see unless he'd shot around the back of one of the buildings.

And then she noticed the sign that pointed out the turn to the Meadowlands Amusement Park. Something tickled deep down in her gut. Before she had a chance to second-guess herself, she drove in that direction. Her GPS told her it was a half hour from town, along a highway bordered by dry grasses and past a few scattered communities where she noted plenty of for-sale signs.

A few more lonely miles with no van sighting and she pulled into a sprawling amusement park lot. The parking shed where visitors would presumably pay for the privilege of leaving their cars during their day of fun was shuttered, but the chains weren't fastened across the entry, so she drove in through the rows of slots marked with peeling yellow paint. The park was closed all right—the rides motionless the towering twists of the roller coasters soaring above the six-foot metal fence with coiling wire affixed to the top and a newish no-trespassing sign. If that wasn't clear enough, the placard underneath read Electrified Fence, though she could detect no indication that it was currently in use.

No van, no other vehicles except for one.

Jack's truck.

Now the tickle in her stomach turned to a squeeze. She dialed the police nonemergency number, which took her to an answering machine. Uncertain, she clicked off before the message finished. Was it an emergency? She would get Jack into trouble surely if her call pulled the police away from their evacuation duties.

She got out, unfastened Arthur's tether and he followed.

Jack's vehicle was locked up as tight as the fencing around the park. Off-limits park and an empty vehicle.

So where are you, Jack?

Arthur planted his paws and barked as a side gate was abruptly opened and a man charged out. Seconds later a security cart roared toward them. She scuttled back and raised an arm to protect herself from being mowed down, realizing how foolish she'd been to try and follow Jack.

Jack heard a bark, which put him into a sprint as he raced around the corner of the fence and the front lot came into view. A man in a security cart zoomed perilously close to Beth, barely stopping short of hitting her.

A slender man in dark pants and polo shirt with a logo on the chest was bearing down on Beth and Arthur also. Jack didn't spare a moment to consider why Beth was at the amusement park when she should have been nowhere near.

He lunged forward with a roar. "Get away from her!"

The man sprang back, surprised, and threw an instinctive punch, but Jack avoided it easily and gave him a shove that sent him falling back against the wire fencing.

He regained his balance, pale eyes spitting fire as he regrouped. Jack could see a set of crooked teeth between thin lips as he fought for breath. Was this someone Jack had known and forgotten? A player in whatever case he was embroiled in? He stayed between the guy and Beth, fists up.

The man pulled out a radio but did not advance again on Beth, who was trying to quiet her dog.

The rotund security guard's bald head was at odds with his thick mustache. He climbed out of the cart. "What's going on here, Mr. Cumberland?"

Cumberland straightened. "Two trespassers. This one shoved me. I was just about to call the police."

"We're in a wide-open parking lot and you both were acting aggressively toward this woman," Jack said before Beth could respond. She finally calmed Arthur and put him into a sit.

The man's brow furrowed. "This is my place and you two are breaking the law by being here. You're in the wrong, not me."

Jack nodded. "I apologize for the trespassing and I'm prepared to be cited for it. Call the cops. Happy to talk to them and straighten it all out."

His look swiveled between them. "Why did you come? Are you together?"

"No," Jack said immediately. "She was just exercising her dog, no doubt. Taking a pit stop or something."

Beth opened her mouth to answer but Cumberland cut her off. "We've had problems with kids sneaking in and causing damage. Sometimes they get belligerent when we confront them. The important point is we're closed as of this afternoon so you need to get out of here and we'll forget the whole thing. Chalk it up to a couple of people who lost their way."

Jack frowned. "Closed? Really? I saw your flyer. Figured you might need help. Are you hiring?"

The man's jaw relaxed a notch as he regarded Jack. "Oh, I see. You're looking for work? Sorry I overreacted. My name's Ray Cumberland. My brothers Wyatt, Daniel and I own Meadowlands." Ray paused for a moment, as if he was expecting Jack to comment, then he shrugged. "Bad timing on your job search because we got word this morning the fire's shifting in this direction so we're closing indefinitely as a precaution."

Time to pull the pin from the grenade before he got

tossed. "That is too bad. I talked to a friend who said nice things about this place. Tess."

Ray jerked. "Tess? The accountant?"

The guard shifted. Jack didn't miss their reactions. He was sure Beth didn't either.

"That's her. Does she work here?"

"No," Ray said.

"Oh, really? I was sure she did."

"Not anymore, I mean. She came aboard recently but she quit. Left a note on Friday and took off." He straightened his polo shirt. "Now that we've cleared up who you are, my apologies, but I have a ton to do to make sure we're ready if that wildfire changes direction. Come back in the summer. We may have work for you then." Ray flicked a glance at Beth, which worried Jack. She wasn't supposed to be involved in any way, shape or form, yet here she was and his story to explain her presence had been flimsy.

Jack held up his palms. "No harm done. We're going."

"You do that. Sorry it didn't work out." Ray Cumberland did not appear sorry in the least. He retreated through a side gate, slamming it closed and keying in a code. They heard the lock engage.

Under the baleful watch of the security guard, Jack got into his truck and Beth in her vehicle. As soon as they were out of view, he drove just far enough until he could pull behind a thick clump of trees. Beth followed suit, parking next to him. He cut the engine and immediately hopped into her vehicle.

"What are you doing here?" he demanded.

She didn't hesitate. "I wanted to be sure you'd left town. I was on my way back to the freeway when I saw the silver van. I lost him until I stopped at a coffee shop where he tried to back into me."

Jack gaped. "He what?"

"I think he was headed here." She pointed back toward the amusement park. "Ray's voice doesn't match the guy I heard, so maybe it was brother Wyatt or Daniel. Your turn. Why did you come here? Are you okay? How's your head? Your vision?"

Tit for tat. "Right as rain, physically. I found a flyer in my wallet. Figured it was the case I was working on."

"Something's going on here. You should hand whatever you've got over to the cops."

He winked at her. "You're worried about me, huh, P.?"

She blew out an exasperated breath. "No, just trying to apply some good sense to the situation. Why are you asking about a woman named Tess?"

"One minute, I want to see what the security guy is up to." Jack pulled a set of binoculars from his pack and Beth extracted one from her glove box.

He chuckled. "Great minds."

"Uh-huh." They stared through the binoculars. Ray had gone but the guard was examining the exterior of the fence and peering at something on the ground in the tall grass.

Beth focused the lenses. "I'm not surprised I arrived to find you in hot water."

"Seems to me like you were the one in hot water." His distraction didn't work.

"I'm waiting, St. James. Tell me the rest."

Why couldn't he shake this woman? He blew out a breath. "I have information indicating I was looking into the whereabouts of a female by the name of Tess. Don't know my contact's full name. All I have is his first initial—A."

She remained staring through the binoculars, fingers tightening around the lenses. "Adam?" Her voice trembled but she cleared her throat. "Is he your contact?"

"I don't know. There's someone else, initial D., which could be the owner-brother Daniel. He could be a source. I still can't remember. That's all I've got."

"You hit a nerve with Cumberland and the guard when you mentioned Tess."

"I thought so too. Ray looked surprised to hear her name."

She strained forward, clenching the binoculars. "Wait. The guard found something."

There was movement in the grass several feet from where the beefy man peered.

"Is that an animal?" Beth said. "There's something wrong with it. It's not walking normally."

The security guard bent, whistling, holding out his fingers. They couldn't see the animal clearly, but when it drew close, the guard shouted and made as if he would kick it, sending the creature yelping in alarm. The guard returned to his golf cart, laughing.

Jack was filled with white hot rage. He reached for the door handle, but Beth clamped both hands around his arm.

"Jack," she snapped, fingernails digging in. "Hold on. He's leaving. Wait one minute. We'll help after he's clear."

His muscles were rigid, stomach churning with disgust. "What kind of a person scares an animal that way?" He fought the urge to sprint to the guard and teach him a lesson, but her tight grip held him in place.

"He won't get away with it," she murmured. "For now, we have to focus on how best to help, which means we don't give up our location. Okay?"

When he managed a nod, she let go.

His anger still felt like a live thing as they continued to observe. The moment the guard guided his cart around the corner and disappeared from view, they crept out of their hiding place. Arthur snuffled at their side. They crouched low, sticking to the trees as much as they could until it was all open space surrounding the parking lot and nothing to do but run and pray the guard didn't return.

In a matter of moments, they neared the fence, both peering around in the thick desiccated grass.

"Where did it go?" Jack whispered.

Beth shook her head. "I don't know. Arthur?"

But the big bloodhound was already plowing through the grass until he suddenly stopped. His thick tail started churning in circles as they hurried over.

At first Jack thought maybe it was a squirrel. Beth put Arthur into a sit and sank into a crouch. Jack took a knee. The animal was brown, smaller than Beth's shoe, with two pointy ears, one tiny brown eye open and the other crusted shut. His right front leg was withered, folded onto his chest, so instead of running away, he was scooting through the earth, getting piled up in dirt and tangled grass. Arthur leaned close to watch as Beth carefully scooped him up, crooning to him.

"It's a puppy, young, maybe a few months old. His leg isn't properly formed," Beth said. "Someone probably dumped him here. I can't imagine how he's survived. He's so thin." She bent closer and talked softly. "Here, baby. It's going to be okay. We're going to get you all fixed up and no one is going to hurt you again, I promise." Her voice was thick with tears and he felt a lump in his own throat.

Arthur crowded close, nosing at the pup.

The dog licked feebly at Beth's chin with a miniscule pink tongue. He was shivering and his plaintive whining was so quiet it was almost inaudible.

Jack put a hand on her shoulder. "Back to the vehicles. Safer there."

They returned to their hiding spot. Beth opened her trunk

for supplies, poured water into a collapsible bowl and placed it on the ground. She held the shivering animal close, nose near the water, but it wouldn't drink. "You've got to be dehydrated. Please, baby. You can do it." She moistened his lips with her finger.

But the puppy still wouldn't drink.

Arthur lumbered close. He gently took the little creature in his mouth and settled it between his two front legs, prodding with his enormous nose. Arthur lapped up some water, which dripped over the little one's head. The pup licked at the droplets and then began to gulp the water from the bowl in frantic mouthfuls.

Jack stood with his jaw hanging open. "Your dog's incredible."

"Yes, he is." Beth patted Arthur. "I knew you were the best dog in the whole wide world, Lovebug."

Jack agreed.

When the puppy's belly was inflated with water, he finally stopped, panting.

"We'll have more in a while, okay?" She wet a square of gauze and washed the dog's injured eye until it gradually opened, revealing a clear brown iris. "There. Isn't that better? You've got a working set. You need a name. How about we call you Peanut?"

Jack scoffed. "No way. Dog that tiny and frail needs a big name. Napoleon."

Beth shook her head. "Ick."

"He's going to have to be tough to survive."

She fingered his delicate triangle ears. The dog looked anything but tough. "Okay. fine, Napoleon it is, but I'm calling him Poe for short."

"So much for a manly name."

"It suits him just fine." Beth scooped up the dog again, wrapping him in a clean towel.

Poe licked Beth's nose, making her giggle.

Something clicked into place for Jack as he watched the two together. He gasped.

Beth jerked a look at him. "What is it?"

"I've seen that dog before."

It was Beth's turn to gape. "How could you? You just got to town."

He pulled out his phone, frantically scrolling through the photos until he came to one that made his breath catch. He turned the screen to her.

It was a blurry selfie of a woman, probably in her mid-thirties, cradling a puppy with a twisted front leg. The amusement park fence showed clearly behind her. The dog in the photo was the same one currently huddled in Beth's arms.

Another fact rose from the recesses of his murky memory.

"You remember something else?" Beth murmured.

He nodded. "I think this is a photo of Tess, the woman I was trying to find."

"The one Ray said quit last week?" Beth's eyes flew wide. "We'll call the police."

"What will they be able to do? There's no way they can search the amusement park with their resources diverted to the wildfire. And it'd be the word of a trespasser with a blurry photo who can't even remember Tess's last name."

Her arms tightened around Poe. "Please tell me you're not thinking what I think you're thinking."

He was already considering the fence, trying to figure out the easiest way. It would have to be after sunset. Lots of time to kill before then. "You need to go home, Beth."

"Absolutely not," she snapped. "Stop this nonsense right now."

"I have to get in there and look around. See if there's any sign of Tess having been there. I have to, Beth." He held up the phone. "My gut says this woman's life depends on it."

She was quiet a moment, stroking the shivering bundle. "Well, tell your gut that first off we're going back to the hotel so I can take care of this pup and you can call the police while we wait for dark."

He thought about it. There was no point in loitering here until sunset, especially if they could make Poe more comfortable elsewhere. "Okay. But if the police won't go in, I will."

She was quiet, rocking the tiny dog as if it was an infant. It made something ache inside his heart, to see her mothering the creature.

"You know what you'd be risking," she said quietly.

"Yes. It's trespassing and I'll be breaking the law. I'm willing to take the consequences of it to help Tess, but you're not going to. If this goes down, you'll wait at the hotel. Call the cops if I don't return."

"I—"

"Beth," he said, his tone leaving no room for disagreement. "I don't need a wingman."

Her eyes blazed blue fire. "That's good, St. James, because you're getting a wingwoman whether you like it or not. The risk is worth it. Now tell me what you're holding back."

He looked straight at her. "I have this feeling…"

His expression sent a chill through her. "What?"

"The woman is in trouble and…" He heaved out a breath. "I think she's Adam's girlfriend."

FOUR

Adam's girlfriend. The phrase continued to loop through Beth's mind ballooning in scope until it eclipsed anything else.

Her son was involved in whatever was happening, as was the woman he loved. Impossible to believe but her gut told her it was the truth. As much as they talked over what Jack could and could not remember, they reached no further clarity.

It was a torturous drive back to the hotel where she was able to book a room next to Jack's. Fortunately, the pet-friendly establishment required only an extra fee and a promise that she'd cover any damages Arthur and the tiny Poe might cause. Not a problem. She'd seen plenty of human guests who had caused way more damage than her fabulously behaved Arthur ever would. And with some protective mats for Poe, he wouldn't be a problem either.

She got the animals settled. Arthur flopped on the cushy mat she'd brought for him. Poe shivered and whined as she tried to wipe him down with a towel. "This isn't going to cut it. I need to give you a bath, little man. You're filthy." But the dog's trembling only increased.

Arthur woofed once and flapped his massive ears.

She took the hint. "All right. I suppose the bath can wait

for an hour or two. Nap first." She nestled Poe on a folded pad and placed him next to Arthur's belly. Poe squirmed and burrowed, sequestering himself deeply under Arthur's love handles.

Beth chuckled. "I think you've been promoted to nanny, Arthur."

Arthur laid cooperatively still as Poe continued his effort to hide himself until only his whip of a tail showed. Arthur sighed when the pup was finally done. Within minutes they were both asleep. She wished she was too, but she doubted she could quiet her somersaulting thoughts.

Mentally she inventoried the boxes in her vehicle, grateful that she'd been toting donated supplies for the shelter collection at the conference. There should be plenty, along with the med kit she always carried for Arthur, to sustain the fragile puppy through their clandestine adventure until they could get him to the vet.

That brought her sharply back to Jack's revelation and the question circling in her brain.

How well did Jack know their son? Was it Adam who'd sent him the photo of Tess?

Jack's rap sent her running to the door.

He eyed the dogs after she let him in. "Didn't take long for them to bond, did it?"

"No. Arthur's a good sport and a natural mother." She gestured him into the chair and folded her arms across her chest. "While they nap, we have plenty of time to clear this all up. Why do you think Tess is Adam's girlfriend?"

His mouth tightened and she saw he was weighing his words carefully. She resisted the urge to hurry him along. "It's still fuzzy, but things are coming back to me," he said. "Very slowly, like those Polaroid photos we used to take that gradually come into focus."

She waited.

"While you were getting the dogs sorted out, I went through the log of recent calls on my phone." He cleared his throat. "I've got several from the contact I listed as 'A' in my address book."

Her heart pounded. "Adam? Did you speak to him?"

"Maybe it's best to let you hear this." He pushed the button for his voicemail. "Listen." He handed her his cell.

Stomach squirming, she held it to her ear.

The recorded message played. "This is Adam Brinkley." The voice was a gentle baritone, deep, slow, like Jack's minus the drawl. She gripped the phone as the recording finished. "Leave me a message if you want a call back. God bless."

When the beep sounded, she stared at the phone until he took it from her and disconnected. Her hands were shaking, her lungs barely working. She'd just heard the voice of her son.

There was no mysterious resonance deep in her soul, an instantaneous riveting connection she'd always imagined she'd feel if she encountered her grown child, but there was something in the tone that brought tears to her eyes. She'd heard Adam speak. The tiny crying baby she'd relinquished was a man. It was hard to catch her breath. "It's him."

He nodded.

Before she could open her mouth to ask a question he stopped her.

"I need to level with you, Beth. While I was in my room I remembered that I looked him up."

"You...contacted him? When?" she heard herself ask over the thudding of her pulse.

"Don't remember exactly but I'd say about four months ago."

She blinked and fought for composure against a rush of emotion. "You mean to tell me you've been talking to our son for months?"

He was on his feet now, pacing the small room. "I know we agreed on a closed adoption, but we're all adults now and there were circumstances in my life that made me rethink things. Only took me a few weeks to find him, once I decided to do it." He tried a smile. "I'm a good investigator."

She didn't smile back. She couldn't explain her own rattling nerves. He didn't have to inform her—why should he? Like he said, they were all adults now and if he wanted to reach out, there was nothing stopping him. Why was she upset? "You've had repeated contact and you didn't tell me?"

"No, I didn't." He rubbed at the knee of his jeans. "From my call records I gather Adam and I talk pretty regularly and we've met face-to-face as well, though I can't remember that too clearly. I have a vague sense of having coffee, going for a walk, that kind of thing." He sighed. "After we'd gotten to know each other, I intended to get in touch with you, but I never made it happen."

Talked. Met. Not a casual acquaintance, an actual relationship. Emotions slammed her with sledgehammer blows. And now Jack was what? Some sort of father figure to their boy? Was she happy about it all? Angry? Sad? It took her a few moments to settle on another feeling—betrayed. "You didn't try very hard to tell me. You could have emailed. Left a message. Written a letter even."

"I…" He sighed. "No excuses. You're right. I didn't try to let you know."

"Why?"

He jammed his hands in his pockets. "To be honest, I'm not completely sure."

Because he thought she'd be unhappy to hear from him?

Or because they both knew she'd not wanted to be a mother when she had Adam?

Why did it slide a blade into her heart? Knowing that he'd done what she'd not been courageous enough to do? The thing she'd yearned for most of her adult life? Find her son and tell him who she was and why she'd done what she did. Tell him it had nothing to do with him, her perfect, beautiful baby. To make it completely, abundantly clear that it wasn't because she didn't love him. She blinked back tears and listened.

Jack talked quickly, as if the words were birds escaping from an overcrowded nest. "I do remember a bunch of random facts about him. He's a great kid, well, if you can call a thirty-eight-year-old man a kid. He's an electrical engineer, like his uncle. His adoptive parents are great too. They live in Indiana, but his mom's sick with lupus. He's working on an offshore oil rig overseas for ten weeks, which probably explains why he hasn't called me back. Never been married, but I finally remembered that he's head over heels for a woman named Tess. She's a freelance accountant and Daniel Cumberland hired her a month ago. She's done most of the work remotely, but she needed to do some auditing on site at Meadowlands."

The details ping-ponged around her heart. Her son had grown up with a loving family. He was successful. He'd found love too, maybe, with a woman named Tess. She squeezed her hands together as Jack continued.

"The next part was fuzzy so I opened a file with some cursory notes." He blushed. "That part about being only a paper-pencil guy wasn't one hundred percent accurate."

Her nod encouraged him to continue.

"The last message Adam got from Tess was Friday and they were accustomed to communicating every day. When she didn't check in, he contacted Meadowlands and they said she was an employee but had abruptly resigned."

"That matches Ray Cumberland's story."

"Yes. Adam also tried to contact her boss, Daniel, but he couldn't get a response. Daniel doesn't live on the property year-round like his brothers, but he was supposedly coming to town for a meeting with them and Tess. Wyatt and Ray stopped taking his calls so Adam called the police. The cops did a welfare check of her apartment but found no signs of violence. Her rent's paid until the end of the month. She stopped the mail. Cops think Tess and Adam likely had a falling-out and she doesn't want to be found."

"Could that be true? Maybe Adam was more invested in their relationship than Tess." It felt strange talking about adult Adam when her only mental picture of him was a dark-haired, solemn-eyed newborn.

Jack shook his head. "I don't think so. My gut says there's something very wrong going on here. Best as I can tell, Adam called me Monday afternoon and asked if I could try to contact her because he can't get back right away." Jack's gaze drifted to the dogs. "She'd told Adam about this stray dog she'd been feeding, trying to catch him so she could get him to a rescue group. She'd left out piles of food and bowls of water. Took a selfie with him."

"Poe?"

"Yes. He must have escaped from her. Adam said she was determined to save him. I don't remember any more specifics."

Beth tried to absorb it. "So you agreed to check it out."

"Don't recall that bit but I'm sure that's what happened. I booked a hotel in town, decided to stop on the way to tell you about my contact with Adam."

"And someone was tailing you, intending to dissuade you from investigating?"

"Seems logical. Guy who whacked me told me to mind my own business and go home."

"And now the park's closed."

"I tried calling Daniel's number again just now, but no one answers. There's no direct line listed on the Meadowlands website for him either, just an email."

"Google search?"

"Age 64, oldest of the three. Runs a tech company. Travels constantly. Doesn't seem to be very hands-on with the park. So you see why I have to get in there. If there's any sign of foul play or a way to contact Daniel, I have to try."

She went to the sink and poured herself a glass of water to give herself a few seconds to process. Emotional storm aside, she was a detective and she had to start thinking like one. "Your plan isn't sound. It's more grasping at straws than anything else. There's a needle in a haystack chance you can find Daniel or Tess by sneaking around the park. If Ray and Wyatt have done something to them, they wouldn't leave any evidence out in the open for you to happen upon."

"I'd head for the office. That's where Tess worked. Maybe I could find her phone, her computer, an indication of what she'd discovered that got her into trouble."

"By breaking in?"

"I was hoping there would be an open gate. I know it's a weak plan at best, but I have to try. If I can sneak in and find another way to contact Daniel, or any lead that proves Tess didn't simply resign, I might have a shot at finding her."

"What about a stakeout? Pending the wildfire activity, you could watch the park for a couple of days. We could track Ray and Wyatt's comings and goings, keep trying to contact Daniel and Tess."

"Or I could simply leave it to the police to investigate when they have the spare manpower, but there's this feeling in my gut, P." He got that quirk in his brow, the one she'd always known meant he was troubled. "And it's telling me Tess is in that park and she's in immediate danger."

He was a good six inches taller so she had to tip her chin up to fix him squarely in her sights. "Police are still the best option. They can get a search warrant. You promised you'd call them before you did anything on your own, remember?"

"Called them first thing when I hit my room. They took a message to give to the lead detective who made the initial inquiries, but with a blurry photo and the fact that I can't even remember her last name, I doubt they'll be rushing over anytime soon. And Adam isn't responding to texts." He paused and blew out a slow breath. "We weren't there for Adam, P. There were good reasons and I'm not casting blame, but we weren't there. Now he needs us. Desperately. I can't tell my son to let the cops handle it while I sit somewhere safe and wait for something to happen."

Weren't there for him. Though the room was warm, cold permeated her body. They had given their son to a family to raise and it had allowed him a bright future. But what if Jack was right and they were Tess's only chance? Could she look Adam in the face some day and tell him they'd elected to leave the problem to someone else?

She refolded the extra dog blankets she'd brought in from her car. "So you figure you'll sneak in, is that it?"

"Yes. Midnight should give me some cover."

"The electric fencing?"

"Yeah, that's a complication. Security guard might leave a gate open or something, but if they engage the electric fence, this plan is probably done before it gets started." He reached out and touched her arm, fingers lingering there, his touch a plea. "Beth, I have to try."

Her stomach quivered at the intensity in his deep voice. She knew he was right. And there was no way she would let him do it alone. Slowly she covered his hand with her, squeezed once, then eased away because it hurt too much to touch Jack St. James. "I'll wait outside with the dogs and call for help if you message me."

He shook his head. "Not necessary, but if you insist…"

"I do."

Their eyes met, his brown and shimmering. "P, don't do this out of guilt."

She swallowed, willing the emotion to stay in check. "This isn't guilt. If you can't stomach telling your son you sat on the sidelines, then you can understand why I have to be part of this too."

Now it was her unspoken plea hovering in the air between them.

"Okay," he said finally.

"And if we lose contact, I'll call for backup and come find you."

His face hardened. "No. If I don't come out, you get clear, call and leave it to the cops."

She straightened ever so slightly to let him know he wasn't making decisions for her. He could make his choices. And she would do the same for herself. "I'll do what I think is best."

"Guess you always do."

What did he mean by that? Did he still feel she'd robbed him of his son? She wanted to ask, but the words simply wouldn't come out of her mouth. The painful subject of Adam stood between them as it always would and she felt the tears threaten again so she drank more water. An awkward silence lingered.

"Hungry?" Jack said. "I thought I'd get some takeout."

The relief at the change of subject left her drained. "No, thank you." Her stomach was churning from his revelation and she just wanted to be alone to sort it out.

"You sure? I'm happy to—"

"Yes," she said, cutting him off. "I'll rest for a while and take care of the dogs. I'll meet you at midnight at our vehicles."

He nodded and left without another word. She collapsed on the bed, depleted.

Adam, her boy, her son. She sifted through all the details she'd learned about him, turning each one over and over in her mind. What had Jack told him about her? That she'd raised a houseful of other children whom she hadn't given away? That she'd been too busy, too guilty, too scared to reach out and contact him while his father had not? She wouldn't cry, because she wasn't sure she would be able to stop and Arthur would feel obliged to get up and check on her. Arthur, the old dog, and his new puppy companion both needed their rest.

And she needed hers.

She lay on her side on the bed and tried to still the thoughts that would not be silenced.

Jack paced the bedroom as the hours passed. He'd eaten the double cheeseburger and fries he'd fetched and now there was nothing to do but watch the TV news reports on the encroaching wildfire and mull over whether or not he'd done the right thing by telling Beth at this particular moment that he'd forged a relationship with Adam. The answer was probably no. Not like that. He'd seen the pain sizzle like a lit match in her eyes and he knew it was the worst timing, but there was no way to keep it from her now. She was already sensing something in the wind and hiding the facts would have only put her more quickly on the trail. She'd dig her way deeper into danger sniffing out the truth and he couldn't allow that to happen.

Guilt nibbled at him. He should have tried harder to tell her sooner. Perhaps even let her know before he decided to make contact with Adam. Though he couldn't remember his exact thought process, he must have decided to come clean with Beth before he set out to find Tess. Maybe he'd wanted her help as a detective? Might he have figured the case would come to her attention with her law enforcement contacts? Or maybe it was a decision born out of prayer.

His thoughts drifted further back into the void. Why had he even made the choice to find Adam at all? Wasn't it a little late in the game to show up on the sidelines? He remembered that reason at least. A friend's sudden death, a hurtful divorce, there were plenty of reinforcers to let him know that he was alone in the world except for the boy he'd fathered.

He'd felt so anchorless, lonely, and thoughts of Adam had begun to infiltrate his every waking moment. Maybe it was a midlife crisis, unless he was too old for that. Beth likely hadn't experienced one of those.

She had a family, children, a lifetime of memories with her late husband. In the future she could look forward to grandchildren, and maybe even great-grands. She had a world of kin and he had no one. Sure, there were friends, some good, some lifelong, but the family piece was missing. His beloved parents were long gone. No siblings, only a brother who'd died before he'd reached the age of two.

For years he'd thought it a problem to be put off for a later date, plenty of decades ahead to wrestle with that issue, and then on his fifty-sixth birthday, his fifty-eight-year-old best buddy up and died on his way to a dentist appointment. Jack had just had breakfast with him that very morning before he was hit head-on by a drunk driver. One minute, alive and flourishing. The next, gone. The days weren't promised. The years had hurtled by. His son was grown. What was he waiting for?

So he'd done it, four months prior unless his sense of time was skewed from the head injury. Snippets from that first contact flashed in his memory. In the course of his journalism career, Jack had been embedded in Afghanistan, fallen into a crevice in the Arctic Circle and jumped out of an airplane with a faulty parachute, and in none of those situations had he been as terrified as when he made the first call to his son.

And he didn't regret one single moment he'd spent with Adam, though he couldn't remember some of them at the present. The thrill of knowing and actually *liking* the man he'd fathered was a profound blessing that Beth might have shared too. But he couldn't impose that on her life when she had made her decision not to reach out.

Made sense to keep it to himself.

But now look what had happened. She believed he'd snuck around behind her back and maybe she was right. *Way to go, St. James.* He was about to push off for another round of pacing when he noticed the light shift under the drawn curtain. As if someone had passed by? On tiptoe he slunk to the side of the drapes and lifted one edge. At first he saw nothing, only the dim yellow pools cast by the parking lot lights.

And then a shadow detached inches from where he was peering and slid slowly along. Someone was sneaking past his room. They'd stopped before continuing. Heading for his truck? Beth's vehicle? His mouth went dry. Her room?

"Not happening, buddy," he breathed. He carried no weapon, but he yanked the Maglite from his pack. It would do.

Because this time Ray, or whoever it was, wasn't going to get the jump on him.

And he sure wasn't going to get near Beth or the dogs.

Gripping the knob, he waited for his moment.

When Poe had begun to stir, Beth fished through the supplies she'd retrieved from her SUV. God had provided once again because there was plenty to choose from. She sprinkled a tablespoon of quality puppy kibble and added a second of a high calorie wet food. While she was at it, she also prepped a half dozen little bags of food to feed Poe while they were in position waiting for Jack. He'd need to eat three times a day at least until he could regain some strength so she intended to be prepared. Since Poe hadn't piddled on the mat she'd tucked under Arthur, she administered an IV with subcutaneous fluids that would help him stay hydrated while his system came back on line. She always carried such supplies in case Arthur needed immediate first aid. It would be the best treatment until a vet could do a full blood panel and exam. He suffered the procedure without complaint.

She thought how eager her kids would be, particularly Kara and Steph, to greet the tiny dog. Poe did not hesitate to gobble mouthfuls of the food, which made her heart sing. Arthur slurped a massive tongue around the bowl to catch whatever Poe had left and she let him. Poe was once again exhausted from the effort of eating, but his stomach was nice and round. Was there anything sweeter than a bulging puppy tummy?

She'd just decided to bathe him and remove any ticks when Arthur shot to the door and began to growl. Something or someone scraped against the outside wall. She froze. Jack? But surely he'd knock, and this was a stealthy sound.

She gave Arthur the hand signal for a silent hold in place. Poe looked around, dazed from his food fest. She prayed he wouldn't let out a whine or yip. Hopefully he'd take a cue from Arthur. If she moved the curtain, the light would shine out and alert the intruder so instead she readied the 9-1-1 button on her phone and got out her pepper spray.

"Stop," came a familiar voice from outside. Jack's.

She flung the door open, spray in hand, to see Jack sprinting through the parking lot, a flashlight raised in his palm like a club. Whoever he was chasing darted away, weaving in and out of the parked cars. Arthur forgot about his hold command and galloped out into the lot, barking furiously. She went after him, calling. She could not have him rushing off into the night. He had no street sense and wouldn't stop for roads or oncoming traffic.

Jack was after someone in dark clothing, likely male, a hoodie pulled over his hair.

"Return," Beth called firmly and Arthur shook himself and obeyed. She clutched his collar.

Jack had drawn abreast of the first parked vehicle when the manager in a hotel uniform slammed the office door open, wielding a shotgun.

She froze.

"Cops are on their way," he roared.

Jack spun around and the manager whipped the gun at him.

"Don't shoot. He's a guest," Beth said. "He was going after someone, an intruder."

The manager looked from her to Jack.

Jack held his palms up, still gripping the flashlight. "Jack St. James, Room 17. Heard someone outside. Guy was casing our vehicles."

The manager exhaled, shook his head and rested the weapon on his shoulder. "Again? Getting like the Wild West around here. I'm going to have to spring for a camera setup."

Beth let out a breath.

"Thieves won't leave me alone," the manager continued. "Cars are busted into continually. They take whatever they can sell quick. What's the world coming to? You two okay?"

Jack nodded and shot a look at Beth, who realized she was still wielding the pepper spray. She tucked it into her pocket and patted Arthur. "All good here. Did he get away?"

Jack nodded morosely. "Ran across the road and into the apartment complex at the other side. Didn't even get a good look at him. Dressed in all black."

"I'll call the cops, but they won't get here anytime soon, and that's certain. Working a couple of blockades due to the wildfire. Sorry for the trouble." The manager trudged back toward his office as Jack joined her, his palm placed protectively on the small of her back.

For some reason, she didn't mind the gesture.

"Guesses about the ID?" he said.

"I didn't hear his voice, but he could be the guy from the coffee shop. He seemed to have a more solid build than Ray Cumberland, but I didn't see him clearly." Tension rippled up her spine at the thought that someone might have been right outside her window, maybe trying to look in, even, while she'd been unaware.

"Or his security guy, but he didn't look fit enough to run that fast." He smiled at her. "Thanks for the pepper spray and dog backup. Appreciate it."

She refused to be charmed by the cocky grin. "It won't do any good to say you should have called the police instead of going after him, will it? One head injury not enough for you?"

He tapped his temple. "Like I said. We're talking pure cement, right here."

She hid her smile as they entered her room. He'd always had that way of lightening the mood. He wasn't quiet and reserved like her husband, Martin, but they both had such a sense of humor. She swallowed, disturbed that she could think of Martin and Jack at the same time. *Business, Beth. Stick to the important points.*

"Why would the Cumberlands come here? Why would they be interested in my car?" It wasn't marked on the side, so her private-eye status wasn't obvious.

"Guessing they were trying to find out who you are. Maybe tamper with the cars? Scare us?"

"Well, that part worked, on me anyway." Her heart was still hammering away. "I was about to give Poe a bath."

He hovered in the doorway. "Need another set of hands?"

"No, I…" She shrugged. "Actually, yes." Was it the fear prickling around her that made her acquiesce? The uncertainty of the situation with Adam and Tess and whoever had been skulking around her hotel room? No, it was pure practicality. Bathing a squirmy pup could be a challenging project and she wanted to be as gentle as possible with the fragile animal.

She rolled up her sleeves and ran warm water in the bath while Jack held Poe. Snatches of his conversation rose above the gurgle of the water.

"You're going to grow up to be a big strong dog, Poe," Jack said. "Don't let anyone tell you otherwise. Doesn't matter how things started out. You're Napoleon St. James and don't you ever forget it."

She stood with dripping hands, watching him. Doesn't matter how things started out? Didn't matter that Poe had been separated from his mom? Discarded? Had their son ever felt that way because of her decision?

Jack locked eyes on her and she realized she'd been silent too long. She lifted a shoulder. "I thought his name would be Napoleon Wolfe."

Jack chuckled. "How about a compromise? We'll call him Napoleon Wolfe St. James. We can share custody." He delivered the pup to Beth and she put him in the tub, holding him upright in the warm water.

"Can you keep him from tipping over while I lather him up?"

Jack knelt next to her and propped up the dog, who yowled as if he was being tortured while Beth rubbed in the dog shampoo. She tried not to pay attention to the feel of Jack's strong shoulder pressed against hers. Arthur crowded in also to be sure his charge would survive the ordeal, taking up a position near the faucet. Rivulets of filth drained from Poe's fur, which she found to be a rich chestnut brown with black ringing his eyes and tipping his pink-lined ears. He was a tiny tot compared to their pack of one-hundred-pound-plus bloodhounds. She counted three ticks clamped onto his tender skin and a long shallow scratch on his belly.

"He seems mostly uninjured aside from malnutrition and the problem of his front leg, which was probably congenital." She wondered if he'd survived partially due to Tess's help. It warmed her inside to think that her son was possibly involved with a woman who loved helpless creatures. All of her children had found mates who adored dogs as much as they did. A blessing.

Jack applied a wet washcloth to the dog's face and received a lick for his efforts. He covered Poe's ears and stage-
whispered. "Fortunate we found him before a coyote did."

"Or the security guard returned."

She heard Jack's teeth grind together as she unstoppered
the drain. Jack handed her a towel and she wrapped Poe
and rubbed him dry. "The bad men won't touch you again,
sweetie. And that's a promise."

Jack held the pup. With tweezers, Beth carefully removed
the ticks and destroyed them, disinfecting the bites with al-
cohol wipes. Poe didn't approve and yelped.

"For your own good," she told him.

She let him plod around on a blanket while they observed.
He hopped and pranced, standing on three legs for a few
moments until he'd tumble over and scramble upright again,
tail zinging back and forth as if he was proud of himself.

"Scrappy," Jack said. "I like that."

"I do too. We'll get him some help in Whisper Valley,"
Beth said. "I know a brilliant vet. She can advise us on the
mobility issue and how to fatten him up. He'll need his shots
and a good flea and tick treatment."

Jack hesitated. "Why don't you take off now then? Poe
needs attention. He shouldn't have to wait any longer."

She arched a brow at him. "Nice try, St. James. Don't
pretend this is about Poe. You're attempting to get rid of
me. Not very subtle."

"No, no way, I mean, well…" He sighed, shoved a hand
through his unruly thatch of dark hair, which only sent it
into more disarray. "It's just that I don't know how the intruder figured out where we were staying. Followed us from
Copper Creek after he clobbered me? Asked around at the
watering holes if anyone had seen us? This undoubtedly
is a small town with loose-lipped locals, but it's not good.

Change your mind, go home tonight with the dogs. It's the smartest choice."

"And leave you to handle things on your own? With Tess missing? And people stalking the parking lots and cafés in town?"

He didn't answer, a stain darkening his shirt where the damp dog had nestled against his broad chest. "It's better that way. I want you to go." His tone was laced with the stubbornness she remembered from their tumultuous past.

She offered up a saccharine-sweet smile. "Well, Jack, we don't always get what we want, now, do we?"

While he appeared to be trying to decide what to say next, she scooped up Poe and guided Jack to the door with a gentle shove. "Now if you'll excuse me, I've got dogs to tend to and it's getting late. Going to clean out Poe's ears and find a sweater for him."

"But—"

"See you soon, Jack. Night night."

After the door closed, she found a pink valentine sweater amongst the donation items. Jack would express disdain but she didn't mind. She and Poe began a wrestling match. He put up a good fight for such a small creature. Jack was right. Spunky. Enveloped in a pink sweater emblazoned with red hearts, Poe gave her a look of pure disdain.

She laughed and set him next to Arthur. "I'm sorry, Poe, but you're cute as a cupcake and there's no getting around that."

Her phone beeped with a text from Garrett.

Checking in. Are you okay?

She thought about what to say. The truth? That she was participating in a dangerous plan with her long-ago boyfriend to save her secret son's girlfriend? If she came clean about those circumstances, all the children would drop their obligations and speed immediately to Copper Creek to escort her safely home and pry every last fact out of her in short order.

And she'd need to explain about why she hadn't gone to the conference, and relate that the stranger had tried to back over her and scoped out her car. And about Adam. She probably should tell her family of trained investigators everything she'd learned. But until she knew more, was it worth it to disrupt her kids and the business?

A-okay, she texted back, praying he wouldn't ask for any details. She wouldn't lie to him, or any of them, but when she got home, she would certainly have a story to tell.

Would it end with saving Tess? Was she really in danger like Jack believed?

In a matter of hours, they might find the answers.

It was a long time until midnight.

FIVE

An ache still sparked from Jack's temple down to his shoulders and he didn't want to admit that his thoughts remained muddled, his reflexes slow. Another round of calls and messages to Daniel and A. on Jack's phone yielded no results. He searched photos and found a few of Daniel, who was a dark-haired man on the short side and slender. He didn't fit the body type for the person who'd clocked Jack and showed up in the parking lot. His snooping revealed that the brothers each kept trailers on the amusement park property.

Jack checked repeatedly out the window of his room and even did some jaunts around the hotel property, but there was no sign the intruder had returned. Ray Cumberland? His brother Wyatt? The unreachable Daniel? Why would any of them take the risk? Had the point been to spy, check in their cars for evidence about who they really were? Certainly Jack's lame excuse about showing up at Meadowlands in search of a job and Beth's coincidental presence wasn't convincing. Or maybe the point had been to send a more permanent message in the parking lot like the one he'd delivered to the side of Jack's skull in Whisper Valley. *Stay away from Meadowlands Amusement Park.*

What had Beth said she'd overheard the van driver saying?

"He'll get the message. You asked me to handle it and I did. If you don't like the methods, do it yourself."

He had a hunch that the brothers knew he was an investigator and had been alerted by some friendly townspeople that he'd been calling around, asking about Tess and the Cumberlands, or that he'd booked a hotel in town. Beth was an enigma they needed to solve.

No concrete proof the attacks were related, of course, but he was increasingly convinced one or more of the brothers wanted him gone. If he was right, the Cumberlands were desperate to hide something. Something going on in the park? The truth about Tess? And why was it impossible to contact eldest brother Daniel?

Throbbing head notwithstanding, Jack was determined to uncover answers that would lead him to the next clue. That was the whole trick to investigating—sifting through tiny pieces of information that led to bigger bits until the puzzle began to take shape. He would get answers eventually. He had no doubt about that.

The more immediate problem was the extremely determined woman in the room next door. If she stuck near him, she was going to be in trouble for sure. Serving as his "wing-woman" on his dangerous endeavor wasn't right. His risk to take, not hers, and he had no doubt her family would agree. He'd seen the protectiveness in them, their obvious love for their mother. He felt a pang of envy. Family was everything. He wasn't going to see hers threatened, even if he had made the mistake of involving her.

Beth, this isn't your fight, at least until I know who the players are.

All that remained was to figure out a way to disentangle himself and make sure she didn't linger in the crosshairs. Protection, that's all he was after. He rubbed his neck. Who was he kidding? Being near Beth awakened some very particular feelings that he did not want to entertain. When he touched her...

Push-ups, ten sets, did not settle his nerves.

He continued pacing the carpet as the hours passed. The clock hit 7 p.m., then 8 p.m. He prayed as he completed the small laps. His brain wasn't firing with its normal rigor so he was going to need direction. Finally, at just before nine, he decided what to do. A quick check out the front door showed him the curtains to Beth's room were closed, the windows dark save for a dim light shining from under the curtain. Hopefully she was resting. Deeply. And the dogs too.

He grabbed his pack, scribbled on the cheap hotel notepad, folded the paper in half and quietly eased from his room. Before he snuck away, he wedged the note under her door. There was no one around in the parking lot, no guests heading in and out of their rooms. He'd caught a break.

Behind the wheel of his truck, he jammed the keys into the ignition and waited until a couple of big rigs approached on the highway. The noise covered the sound of his engine turning over. Hopefully. Lights off, he eased out of the parking lot. A glance out the rearview reassured him that her room was still quiet, the curtains closed.

Score one for his covert skills.

His plan was still the same; it would just commence earlier, without Beth and the dogs. If things went his way, he'd find some evidence Ray was lying about Tess's abrupt resignation, or at least some morsel of information that would lead him to some next steps. He would leave the park before Beth even knew he'd vacated the hotel. It was a tall order. He'd better make the best of his three-hour head start.

She'd be furious. He smiled, thinking about how her eyes would spit fire and spots of color would infuse her cheeks like a fall sunrise. He'd always thought Beth's fury made her the most beautiful woman in the world.

Had her husband thought so too? Undoubtedly. He wondered about what kind of man Martin Wolfe had been. Strong, without question. Beth would choose a worthy counterpart. Honorable. She'd settle for nothing less. It gave him a pain under his sternum to think about how she'd crafted a beautiful family with Martin, five kids who obviously adored her, but he was happy about it too. Happy, and sad for himself.

What had he to show for his fifty-seven turns around the planet? A nice condo with a music collection he listened to by himself, for the most part. A sprouted avocado pit with a six foot vine, the only green thing in the place. An ex-wife with whom he had no contact and a couple of girlfriends who'd lost his number on purpose or he theirs. None of his relationships stuck.

Because none of them held a candle to Beth.

He immediately shook that thought away. It was simply one of the ridiculous daydreams he'd held on to over the years. She wasn't his. She never was and never would be, but during occasional sleepless nights, he allowed himself to stray to the "what could have beens." Deadly and depressing. God didn't want him to dwell in the past.

Each bump and creak of the truck flared his headache, so he grabbed a bottle from his pack, one-handed, and swallowed two aspirin with a swig from his water bottle. When he drew close to the park he turned the lights off and rolled in the dark to the same hideaway where he and Beth had parked to rescue Napoleon. Plenty of shrubbery around to conceal him...unless someone was diligently looking. In that case, he was doomed to fail.

The chill poured over him as he got out and eased the

door shut behind him. Baseball cap pulled low over his brow, he didn't even turn on his penlight as he made his way to the front of the park. Before he left the cover of the tall, parched grasses, he crouched for a moment, assessing, heart beating double-time. The fence—was it juiced up? Not enough to kill him but it would cause sufficient pain to prevent him climbing it. As he hurried close, he listened carefully, hearing no soft buzz of electricity humming through the coils. He grabbed a stick and flicked it against a wire, braced for a shock. Nothing. Not activated. He'd gotten a break. At last.

The front entrance was too visible in the smoky moonlight and clearly locked tight. He was on his way to the side gate where he'd seen Ray emerge before, when a sound sent him scuttling back in the shadows.

On his cart, the security guard was approaching from inside the gate Jack had just been about to try. As Jack watched, the man stopped, climbed from behind the wheel and punched in a code on a small keypad. The gate clicked, he shoved it open and then edged his vehicle through. Jack was crouched a mere five feet from the guard, motionless.

The guard then trudged back, pulled the gate closed, and unclipped his radio from his belt. "Yeah, I'm doing my rounds and then my buddy's picking me up at the main gate for my dinner break. I'll leave the cart there. Be back in an hour."

Jack perked up at the opportunity—an hour without having to dodge security. Even better, he noticed the gate hadn't fully latched and the guard didn't check behind him before he motored off. It was almost closed, but not all the way. There was a gap of an inch, no more.

Perfect. Access and an hour of snooping before the guard returned. Hopefully the brothers were sound asleep in their trailers. He couldn't have asked for more.

When the guy in his cart rattled around the corner of the fence, heading toward the front, Jack hustled through and examined the keypad inside that allowed access. He didn't want to find himself trapped, so he yanked off his hat and stuffed the bill of the cap in the lowest hinge. The gate would appear to be closed, but the obstruction would work to keep the lock from fastening fully, allowing him to sneak out again before the guard returned. The countdown had started.

Get moving.

The darkness was complete, for the most part, but enough safety lights shone to allow him to orient himself. He'd done some online recon already. Four "lands" in the park, following the themes of jungle, mountain, ocean and desert. Plenty of rides, snacks and kiosks populated each one. To his left, a series of squat buildings, painted banana leaf green, announced the jungle motif. A plastic giraffe protruded from the top of the Safari Spinner, a giant circle of swings that whirled patrons in a dizzying orbit. To his right, a path led to the roller coaster, bumper cars and fun house. The brothers' trailers, he'd discovered from a Google Earth search, were buried deep on the sprawling property, in the back lot with storage and an electrical shed. There was an office building there too and that's where he had the best chance of finding any trail that could lead him to Tess. If he found any evidence of wrongdoing, it would be inadmissible and he'd likely go to jail himself, but if he could find something to convince the cops Tess was in trouble, it would be worth it. At least it might provide a hint of where to look next.

Best to stick to the paths at least until he got to the "employee only" area and the office.

The park encompassed some thirty acres, the kind of place he would have loved under other circumstances. A lingering scent of popcorn and french fries hung in the air along with something sweeter, a hint of caramel or cotton candy. It brought him back to one of his first dates with Beth.

"If you're not too scared, we can go on the Ferris wheel." He'd hoped to have an excuse to snuggle up and put a protective arm around her.

"Not the Ferris wheel. Too slow. Come on." She'd taken his hand and tugged him to a roller coaster that left him almost losing his lunch by the end. Not Beth. She'd emerged with cheeks ruddy and eyes sparkling like agate, her laughter so merry and light it took his breath away. Maybe he'd fallen in love with her that moment. Certainly his heart had never beat exactly the same way again. Then dates had turned into a relationship that sped way too fast and way too free. How had it all gone so wrong?

At least Adam hadn't suffered because of their mistakes. Though the particulars were still foggy, he had the overwhelming sense that Adam had lived a good life, with loving, stable parents. *Thank you, God.*

He came upon a map on a signboard alongside the path. Best to double-check since he couldn't afford to lose his way. Exactly as he'd anticipated. Heading along Adventure Trail should allow him to skirt the lagoon for the boat ride and take him on the most direct path to the back lot.

As he moved deeper along the paved route there were lampposts for overhead illumination, but most of them weren't operating. Cost savings since the park was closed? Risky to activate his Maglite, so the additional glow of the crescent moon would have to suffice. Too bad it was rapidly becoming obscured by a layer of acrid smoke.

The overgrown landscaping told a story. What had once been neatly spaced clumps of foliage had grown together in tangled heaps that encroached on the walkways and threatened to swallow up signage. Tough times for the entertainment businesses? Economic hardship might have necessitated cutting back on nonessential services. With many families tightening their belts and inflation continuing to push up prices, running an amusement park facility had to be a sketchy proposition. The expenses would be killer. Had Tess found evidence of wrongdoing on the part of the brothers?

He passed a neon yellow Thrilla Gorilla ride, which was a massive propeller-type mechanism that catapulted guests through the air. A net underneath caught all the belongings that no doubt rained out of their pockets. He could imagine the screams. Beth would love it. His eyes drifted to the still metal machine, the series of bolts gleaming silver.

A suspicion crept into his thoughts. Cutting corners on the landscaping would be one thing…but what if the brothers had begun finding other ways to save money? The rides were required to be inspected by officers of the state or county, but it wasn't beyond imagination that an official could be bribed, or false maintenance records created to imply safety was up to snuff. Perhaps Tess had become aware of crooked activity and brought it to Daniel's attention? Had Daniel hired her because he suspected his kin? Where was he?

He jogged along the path, steering clear of the encroaching plants, the possible theory materializing further. What if two of the three brothers were cutting dangerous corners? Or stealing profits they weren't entitled to? Tess might have revealed that in her audits, which would have made her a liability, so they dealt with her, made up a story that she quit. Perhaps Daniel didn't believe his brothers' explanation that Tess had abruptly quit and they had disposed of him too.

Wild theory? Or credible theses?

The image of the woman cradling the emaciated dog they'd come to know as Poe surfaced. A woman like that wouldn't have walked away from wrongdoing, tucked her tail and run. She'd have told Daniel and failing that, the cops. Talked it over with Adam at least. Had Adam told Jack of any specific allegations? He simply could not recall.

A cold shiver ran up his spine and he zipped his jacket higher. *Lord, please let me find Tess if she's in trouble.*

Jack checked the clock on his phone. He'd been in the park for fifteen minutes. It was moving along toward ten when the guard would return. The hours until Beth would head out to meet him were speeding by, too. The whole mission had to be completed before she had a chance to involve herself again. He picked up the pace.

The path curved past the Thrilla Gorilla, a towering wood-framed roller coaster that soared one hundred feet at its peak before it spiraled into death-defying dips and turns. The wood slats creaked and groaned in the wind. At the ride's entrance was a snack shack with a roof made to look like rushes and tables painted bright green, though the paint was chipped and worn in places. He hurried past a machine that offered to provide a souvenir penny for a fifty-cent deposit. He shook his head at that one.

The scuff of a heel on the gritty path made him whirl around.

The security guard stepped out from behind the machine, grinning. His name tag shone in the lamplight. Bud.

Jack's heart sank. Captured.

"Surprised to see me? It's Jack, right? Jack St. James?" Bud said.

"Yes," he said, nonchalantly. "How'd you find that out?"

The guard quirked a brow. "I got all kinds of fancy skills. What are you doing here, Jack?"

"Just taking in the scenery and all." He fisted his hands, ready for a fight.

"Uh-huh." The guard chuckled. "You know, you're not as smart as you look for an investigator."

He stayed quiet, running through possible escape scenarios.

Bud chuckled. "You think I'm such a dork that I'd leave the gate open by accident?"

Jack kept his fighter's stance, stomach sinking as he realized how easily he'd been duped. He'd underestimated the security guard and now he was going to pay for it unless he could figure a way out. "Nah. Just figured you were lazy."

The grin vanished. "Not lazy. Waiting for you to try something dumb like this. Boss told me you were holed up in town with your lady friend so I was expecting another visit."

Your lady friend. How was he going to keep Beth out of it now? Sweat broke out on his forehead but he kept his voice calm. "She's an acquaintance, nothing more. She's leaving town this morning. Maybe already gone."

Bud's jovial tone dropped away. "Be good for her if she was."

Plans, Jack. Now. Jack didn't think the guard looked to be in great shape. He still had a chance to handle it with a rapid fistfight unless the guy had already called for backup. He eased forward to the balls of his feet while the guard kept talking.

"My boss doesn't like spies," Bud said.

"Who's your boss? Ray Cumberland? Wyatt? Daniel maybe? All of them?"

"Everybody wants to be a boss around here, but Ray's

happy leaving things to Wyatt and they both trust me to get things done."

"Not Daniel? You don't take orders from him?"

The guard's eyes narrowed. "He doesn't even live on the property. Off running his highfalutin tech business. Pops in once in a blue moon when he's feeling bored."

"And takes in a share of the profits."

"That's the way a family business is supposed to work, isn't it? Everyone gets a piece of the pie." Bud shook his head and whistled. "I'm gonna get a raise for this. I saw you testing the electric fence, moving around to the side gate. Nice trick I played there, huh? Saying I was going to be gone for an hour. Drove around the back and let myself in. You bought the hook, the line and the sinker, didn't you? Hilarious."

He had. Some investigator. Self-recrimination would have to wait. Jack eased to the side to line up his punch. One to send him reeling, another to knock him out. "What exactly is going on in this place that your bosses are so desperate to keep anyone from finding out, Bud?"

"Nothing in this park concerns you, my man."

"It does if there's a missing woman. Tess is her name and she worked here until she supposedly quit without notice. You know something about that, don't you? Better to come clean and protect yourself because the police know. They'll be here anytime."

Bud's mouth tightened. He did know something. Jack felt a stir of excitement until Bud removed a stun gun from his belt and flicked it to life. "Bluffing isn't going to work, Jack. The cops aren't on their way. You don't know anything and you never will. Should have taken off when you had the chance."

Jack bolted, trying to dive to the side, but his reflexes were slowed by his concussion.

Bud lunged with the Taser, connected with Jack's forearm.

Electricity sizzled through his body—waves of agony—and the ground rushed up to meet him.

Beth drove fast, fueled by fury. Arthur in the back seat was alert to her mood, nose sniffing in her direction. Poe was bundled in a box anchored on the seat next to Arthur. She didn't have a tether that would keep the miniscule dog in place, nor a harness small enough to accommodate his four-pound frame, but she hoped Arthur would prevent Poe from hopping out of the box if the puppy got the notion. Arthur had excellent common sense, which was more than she could say for Jack.

Her knuckles were white on the steering wheel and she had to force herself to unclench her jaw and slow to the speed limit. *He must have actually sustained a brain injury if he thought it was a good idea to sneak off without telling me.*

His note read:

Change of plans. No need for backup. Contact you soon and we'll have that weird green tea you like. J

That weird green tea she liked—matcha—she'd shared with the boy she'd loved, Jack, in a tiny hole-in-the-wall café near the college where she'd been enrolled for precisely half a semester. How grown-up they'd felt, high school graduates, her a new college student and him a poorly paid intern at a local newspaper taking night classes. Grown-up and heedless of consequences and unfettered by commandments they'd thought of as outdated rules instead of protections. They'd been playing at being grown-ups until she'd gotten pregnant. Then reality had rushed in like floodwaters and washed away anything that remained of their childhood. Two minimum wage earners. Her with an estranged, disinterested family and him with a rigid father whom he could never please.

Marriage, as Jack had proposed? They couldn't get through the week without having a tiff or overdrawing their bank accounts. Too young, too foolish, too irresponsible, too far from God.

And it looked like Jack hadn't shed his impulsive tendencies, taking off without her, leaving some flimsy excuse as if he thought she wouldn't see right through it. Her stomach roiled.

She should have known. Maybe subconsciously she did, which was why she'd checked the parking lot at nine thirty and found Jack's truck gone. He'd acted without her, just like he'd done in seeking out their son. The hurt of it bubbled afresh. No matter what her reaction, he should have told her—that much she knew. A wound she'd carried for thirty-eight years had broken open, and she wasn't sure how to bind up the ragged edges. Adam, the son she hadn't kept. The one she hadn't even contacted.

The hazy darkness held the bitter scent of burning grass and the radio alerted her that the scope of the wildfires had grown to gobble thousands of additional acres. An even more compelling reason why they should have gone straight to the police in the first place and never even entertained Jack's reckless plan.

The image of the woman with Poe flashed in her mind. There was something tender about her expression in the photo that spoke of a loving heart, a sincere nature. Beth swallowed a lump in her throat. If Tess was the woman Adam loved and he'd been frantic to find her, he'd called the one person who could help. Jack St. James. That trust was precious and she realized she was grateful for their bond.

Only Jack needed someone beside him, and strange as the notion was, she knew there was no one else for that job but her. Together they'd made a child and together they'd save the woman Adam loved, if she truly was in danger.

She pushed to the maximum speed until she turned into the long entrance to the amusement park and rolled toward the place where they'd sequestered on their last visit. Through the grass she backtracked along the trampled trail they'd made before, from which they'd spotted Poe. She wasn't surprised to find Jack's truck parked there.

She pulled in beside it, texted him and waited.

No response.

She texted again.

Still nothing.

Her pulse pounded. She didn't dare call him in case he hadn't remembered to silence his phone.

Would it be best to contact the police? But her phone had no bars and really how could she do that anyway without causing Jack to be arrested for trespassing?

Which was exactly what *should* be happening. This reckless plan was bound to lead to disaster. She snatched up her night vision binoculars and scanned. Quiet. Dark. No sign of the security guard, just the fence gleaming in the darkness. Jack would have sought out the side entrance. She'd have to get closer to see if she could spot him.

Poe shifted in his box and the reality hit her. Dogs. She now had two of them. There was no way she could leave baby Poe alone and Arthur's skills might prove crucial.

"Okay, boys. Field trip." She picked up Poe and deposited

him in the deep front pocket of her jacket. "You're going to have to stay in silent mode, okay?"

Poe burrowed down into the depths, creating a warm ball next to her stomach. Hopefully he'd take a nice, long nap.

After she unclipped him, Arthur trundled out, poked his nose into her pocket to be sure his ward was secure and looked at her expectantly as she pulled on her backpack. She gave him the silent command, pushed the SUV door closed and they set off, scuttling as fast as they could manage to the front entrance and around to the side gate. She stuck to the cover of the shrubs that would conceal her unless someone was looking carefully. Still no sign of the security guard. She tried texting Jack again but this time the message refused to send. "Must be in a dead zone," she grumbled.

Through the chain link, she peered into the darkened interior. Smoke thickened the air around them, tingling her skin, burning her eyes. The wildfire was a growing monster. Another reason to speed things along.

She risked moving closer. Arthur angled his nose to the metal, but she didn't let him touch it. It didn't appear to be electrified, but she took a plastic spoon from her pack and tapped it since she wasn't certain.

No buzzing, so hopefully no shock. At least that was going in their favor. But why wasn't Jack responding to her texts?

Arthur rumbled in his throat, trying to tell her something. She looked closely as he snuffled again at the gate, tail erect. What was he after?

She shaded her penlight with her palm and shone it on the ground where Arthur snuffled. An object impeded the gate from fully closing, a detail that hadn't been obvious from farther away. Her throat constricted as she recognized Jack's baseball cap wedged above the lower hinge.

"Good job, Arthur." She could hardly breathe as she stared at the clue he'd left behind. *Jack, what have you done?*

She struggled with the choices.

Keep trying to text Jack?

Drive away until she could get a signal, then call the police?

Arthur stiffened. She heard voices coming closer and she and the dogs scuttled back to the cover of the shrubbery.

Two men charged into view, one slightly taller and thinner than his stockier companion. Ray, she recognized.

"We can't risk him telling anyone." It was a voice she'd heard before, the man on the phone who'd tried to run her down. Ray's brother? Wyatt?

"What about…?"

She missed the end of the comment.

Wyatt replied. "We can get it on our way out of town."

Can't risk him telling anyone…

Were they talking about Jack?

"We've got enough problems. And who was the lady with him? Maybe she sent them the files," Ray said.

Files? Alarm bells clanged in her mind.

"Bud says he took care of the problem. If they're investigating, then they don't have proof yet. We still have time to pack up our stuff, get to the bank in the morning and take off."

The two men were so close that she could hear their feet whisking over the dry grass. Within moments they'd be around the corner and they couldn't fail to realize the side gate was open. They'd know Jack was inside.

What's more, she couldn't make a run back to where she'd hidden her vehicle without being spotted. She would be discovered too. Three seconds or less, to make the decision. Run for the car? Call the police and hope the call went through? Neither plan was likely to succeed.

And Jack's life might be hanging on her decision.

She thought it over for one more moment before she darted through and into the park, Arthur at her side, removed Jack's cap and eased the gate closed.

Decision made.

She hoped it wouldn't prove to be a disastrous one.

SIX

Lightning fast she ran with Arthur, ducking behind the nearest structure, a hot dog vendor cart. Arm around her dog, the other patting the bundle in her pocket, she panted, praying the brothers hadn't spotted her.

The two men pushed through the gate a moment later. She heard it close, completely this time, locking into place with a foreboding clang. Ray mumbled something. She couldn't decipher the words over the blood pounding in her temples, but the intensity was unmistakable. She could see the second man better now, with his stockier, more brutal build. He was undoubtedly Wyatt Cumberland and definitely the one who'd menaced her at the coffee shop. As she and Arthur watched, they broke into a run and disappeared along a darkened path in the park's interior. Two men on a mission.

She remained hidden for a beat struggling to catch her breath. Poe squirmed in her jacket. Quickly she texted Jack. The message wouldn't send. *Next move, Detective Beth?*

Ray and Wyatt had rushed off with urgency; there was no mistaking that.

Did it mean Jack had been found out?

A blinking blue light inside the gate caught her attention. When she was fairly certain the brothers weren't coming back, she hurried close to check, spotting a keypad she hadn't noticed before with a digital readout: Locked and armed. Ray had seen to it that the door was now activated... from the inside? If she tried to get out, they'd be alerted in an instant. Trapped. Why?

The brothers were intent on controlling who entered their park...but also who was able to leave. Had Tess stumbled onto whatever it was and they feared she'd reveal her findings to Daniel? To Jack?

Arthur waggled his tail, asking about their next move. Great question.

She caressed the dog. "Looks like Mama got us stuck in here." With a little resourcefulness, she might be able to find a section of the fence where it was possible to climb over. There had to be a ladder lying about, but it would be difficult carrying Arthur and Poe. Perhaps all the exits weren't secured in such a way, with a keypad requiring a code to unlock. Didn't really matter at the moment. She couldn't leave until she tried to find Jack because deep down, her dread was increasing by the second. Once more she tried her phone and again found it unable to send messages or make calls. So she'd have to find him on her own. She hadn't seen which path the brothers had taken so following them was off the table.

The grounds were vast and there was no way she could locate Jack quickly, but she had a faithful companion who could. Bloodhounds were better than any tracking app on the most high-tech phone. She bent and patted Arthur before holding Jack's baseball cap to the dog's nose. "Arthur, find."

The dog immediately glued his muzzle to the ground and trotted toward the nearest path. Beth's nerves tightened. Arthur would locate Jack she had no doubt. Unharmed? *Please let him be okay, Lord.* That maddening man...

Arthur moved as efficiently as the younger dogs in their

family, at least for short bursts. She had to jog to keep up. He passed the Thrilla Gorilla and stopped near a small snack shack. He circled, looped and sniffed.

She risked a glance with her flashlight, shielding it with her palm. The ground was well trodden, packed by the dry season into an anvil of hard earth unsoftened by any friendly rain, but her light caught the source of Arthur's fascination—two parallel ruts that ended where the grass started.

Heel marks? As if someone had been dragged. Her breath caught, but Arthur was already moving again, rejoining the path where it meandered to Mountain Mayhem, an area of the park done in an alpine theme, complete with an abominable snowman roller coaster, one of the premier attractions. "One of the last remaining historic wooden coasters," the sign read. Arthur stopped several times, wandering, circling, fastening on the scent again. The dog's occasional redirecting made Beth suspect there was a vehicle involved, perhaps a golf cart? Bloodhounds couldn't follow a scent if the object sped away in a car, but if Jack had been forced into an open-air cart, Arthur would still be able to track him.

Arthur loped on, moving ever more confidently to the snowman coaster. Rising some one hundred fifty feet into the air, it loomed above them, menacing, as if it was waiting for a victim to climb aboard. Below the towering ride with its latticework of beams and iron rails was a cement platform, one end of which was where the guests would be strapped into their compact red cars. Underneath the platform was an enclosed space, stretching on for a half mile. It formed a long wooden tunnel that she imagined covered the inner machinery and storage areas. What else did that big structure conceal?

The smoke particles danced in the air around her, further adding to the gloom. She wondered if there was a network of concealed pathways all around the park that enabled workers to move about unseen by the visitors. Had Jack been snatched unawares?

They'd drawn adjacent to the coaster's enclosed underbelly. Ribbons of paint peeled away from the walls like diseased skin. Now that she was close, she detected two doors crafted to disappear seamlessly into the facade. Both were fastened with padlocks. The metal was weathered by wind, rain and sun, but the locks held firm.

Arthur looked at her, circled twice more and even pawed at the first door.

Jack's inside, Arthur said with his body language as clearly as if he'd spoken aloud. *Let's go get him.*

Jack clearly had been imprisoned. Fear made her skin clammy. "I believe you, Arthur. Just trying to figure out how to get in." She darted a look around, tried her phone again—no signal.

No help coming for Jack. Beth and the two dogs were all he had.

She knew the wise action would be to continue looking for a way out of the park, a means to summon the authorities, her family, but as she looked into Arthur's brown eyes, she knew Jack was in trouble. She knew it deep in her gut and so did her dog. If she was wrong, she'd take the consequences, pay the penalty for breaking and entering. But she wasn't wrong and she wasn't going to let him die in there.

In a moment she'd slipped the small pry tool she always kept on hand from her pack. It served an endless variety of purposes but this was the first time she'd used it to bypass a locked door without the owner's permission.

The act could lose her her investigator license. So be it. It took no more than a few tries before the hinges of the lock popped off. She caught the chain before it crashed to the ground, settling it behind a nearby bucket filled with rusted nuts and bolts. Arthur was already pushing at the door with his front paw, but she held him behind her as she eased into the darkened interior.

The smell of mold and diesel assaulted her. The air felt damp, and the wood walls were tacky with moisture. She held Arthur in place with a command, waiting for her eyes to adjust. They didn't. The pitch black was unrelieved by windows and she couldn't feel any handy light switches so she risked flicking on her flashlight. She was in a cramped space, maybe ten by ten and no more than seven feet high. The cement floor was cracked and speckled with stains of various colors. No sign of Jack.

"Arthur, find."

The dog scampered to the far end of the space where she hadn't noticed the outline of another door with a rusted iron handle. She hurried and yanked it open. Inside was a narrower passage, same walls and floor but slanting down like a sort of tunnel that led into the darkness where her light couldn't reach. Catacombs underneath the coaster. She hadn't anticipated that.

Cold air prickled her skin to goose bumps. "Jack?" she whispered into the void.

She heard nothing, but Arthur didn't need to rely on his hearing as he flapped his ears at her.

"Is he that way?"

Arthur pranced and pawed, eager to be given the signal to go.

A cobweb trailed across her cheek, making her shiver. She gave the dog a silent command to move slowly, which was completely against his natural inclination. To his credit, he kept to a creep. They moved several paces deeper into the passage.

"Jack?" she called again softly. Arthur was trained to find survivors, but there had been a few cases where he'd located those who hadn't made it, their attempted rescue morphed into a recovery. Those were the hard cases, the terrible moments that stuck with her and maybe with Arthur too. What if it happened now?

No, she told herself. That wasn't possible. Jack St. James was alive and they would find him. They moved deeper into the darkness.

She heard a groan.

She and Arthur darted forward in unison.

At the end of the passage where the space widened into a storage room, she let Arthur lead the way. Left, he indicated, behind a pile of moldering pallets.

Arthur flopped down next to Jack, who lay on his back, unmoving.

With a murmured prayer, she ran to him.

Jack swam into consciousness to discover a golf ball-sized nose skimming his cheeks and chin. Warm dog breath enveloped him.

A feminine voice called off the dog and cool hands brushed over his temples and peeled the tape from his mouth.

"Beth," he gasped, finding her so close he could have kissed her. Instead he looped his bound wrists around her shoulders and pulled her to his chest. "You shouldn't have come." But her warmth felt like a blanket, wrapping him in comfort. He pressed his mouth to her cheek and took in the satin of her skin and the wild beating of her heart. Overjoyed as he was to see her, he cringed knowing she'd just put her life at risk to find him.

To his great surprise, she kissed him and quickly extracted herself from his hold. Good thing because he'd likely have wanted that kiss to go on forever.

"You're trying my patience." Her voice trembled. "Running off like that."

She sat on her knees and set the flashlight on a box. He heard her swallow, a small gulp. "Honestly, I'm so relieved to find you alive that I can't even give you the proper tongue-lashing you so richly deserve."

"It's okay. Arthur is handling that." Indeed the dog had managed to simultaneously back off as his master commanded and snake out his giant tongue and apply it to Jack's forearm. He didn't mind. He felt like he was lying on an iceberg.

Her hands glided over his head, searching for injuries. Her palms were so soft and soothing he wanted to close his eyes and sink into her care. Instead he gathered himself and sat up with a grunt. "We've got to stop having you finding me incapacitated," he grumbled. "It's embarrassing. Where are we?"

"In the tunnels under the giant roller coaster. Arthur tracked you and I pried the lock off the outer door."

He let that sink in.

She touched a sore spot on his arm. "Burn?"

"Taser."

"Guard?"

"Yep. Bud's his name. Set me up neat as anything, I'm humiliated to admit. Told me he works for Ray and Wyatt. Daniel is an absentee brother, but that doesn't mean he isn't a part of whatever is going on here."

"I don't think so. I heard Ray and Wyatt talking. They're afraid Tess was going to report something incriminating to Daniel in a meeting tomorrow or that we'll find something out we shouldn't."

He frowned. "They might have killed him."

"I don't know, but one or both of them ordered Bud to lay the trap for you."

"I owe Bud, that's for sure." His shoulders were in agony with his wrists cinched together in front of him with zip ties. "Can you cut these?"

She extracted a Swiss Army knife from her supplies and sawed through the plastic restraints, which no doubt Bud must have applied after he'd used the Taser. Jack's ribs ached, which indicated he'd been treated none too gently. *We're going to have a word when I find you, Bud.* After his hands were free, he chafed them to restore the circulation. "What time is it?"

"Almost eleven."

"You were supposed to let me handle things."

"Uh-huh. Would've served you right if I left town. That might have taught you a lesson."

"Part of me wishes you did, P. We're in deep now." All of them were.

"That's true. I couldn't get a signal to call the cops before we found you and I don't have one now. It's like the park is a dead zone."

"Does your family know you're here?"

After a tiny pause, she shook her head.

Of course. She hadn't told them everything about Jack, a reminder of her embarrassing past. That spoke volumes. He didn't blame her but it stung anyway. In case she hadn't noticed he was a grown-up man now, not an adolescent mistake. Bigger fish to fry, at the moment.

The nasty fact was that no one knew they were under attack at the Meadowlands Amusement Park. He kept the worry from his expression.

She told him about how she'd sprinted through the fence

a moment before Wyatt and Ray. "They didn't see me sneak in, but it was close. They were in a huge hurry."

"Bud probably told them he got the drop on me. I don't know if they helped him dump me here or if he did it himself." He stood, wobbly-kneed but determined not to show it. "We have to start moving because they'll be looking. Get you and the dogs away."

"Away how? The gate I entered is locked from the inside. The brothers have control, I assume."

He considered through his pounding head, his mouth dust dry. Wordlessly, she handed him a water bottle. The gesture stopped him. She'd always been able to do that, predict what he needed before he'd said a word. She'd known he'd want to keep the baby, that he'd suggest they get married. And she'd known they'd never have made it work. He gulped the liquid to soothe his dry throat and wash the memory away.

"Back where their trailers are there's a gate for deliveries. It's less visible than the one in front. We'll make our way there. It's not as secure, but if it's armed like the rest of them, there's a utility shed close and maybe we can disable the system. If that fails there's a good likelihood of a nearby vehicle we can use to drive right through, gate or no gate. So far the fence isn't electrified and we'll hope it stays that way. I'll help you climb over with the dogs if that avenue presents itself. You'll leave and I'll—"

"Leave too," she commanded.

Nope. All the facts made him feel dead certain that Tess was a threat to the brothers. If she was still alive she was in grave danger and he wasn't clearing the scene until he was totally sure she wasn't being held on the premises. He decided to tackle that problem later. "Where's Poe?"

She patted her bulging pocket and Poe periscoped up into view.

Jack chuckled. "His first mission."

"Hopefully not his last."

That was sobering. Taking a risk with his own life was one thing. Now he was responsible for Beth and two dogs as well. He struggled to his feet with a helping hand from Beth. Once upright, he thumped a beam that was less than a foot from the crown of his head. "This structure underlies the whole roller coaster platform, spans a good half mile. I remember looking up the blueprints."

"What else do you remember?" She didn't look at him as she repacked her supplies.

"Just what you already know."

"That you went ahead and contacted Adam without telling me and he asked you to find his girlfriend."

He felt her hurt and his own response—guilt and the slightest bit of anger. "Should have told you about Adam long ago, yes, but I didn't need your permission to find him."

Her chin went up for a moment and then dropped. "I wouldn't have discouraged you. I..." She trailed off with a shrug. "I'm not sure why I feel upset about it."

Maybe he shouldn't have come off so forcefully. She deserved some grace, especially since she hadn't had more than a few hours to process that Adam was both back in Jack's life and his girlfriend was missing. "It's a lot to assimilate and you have had nothing but chaos so I get it."

She didn't answer, but her shoulders relaxed.

He changed the subject. "This building we're in extends underneath the coaster in exactly the direction we need to travel to reach the trailers."

"So you're thinking we move underground."

"Might as well. I think this tunnel should emerge facing the back lot. At that point we're out in the open, but the less distance we're in view the better. Wyatt and Ray are no doubt getting briefed by Bud about his heroic takedown and hopefully that will gain us a little time. Far as they know, I'm locked in, unconscious. They aren't aware you're here…" He paused. "Unless the cameras are online. I passed several that didn't appear to be live, but that could change."

Her mouth tightened. "If that's the case, we're just going to have to pray they don't check the feed anytime soon."

"Agreed. The more prayers the better."

She cocked her head at him. "Back in the day neither one of us would have cared much for prayer."

He smiled. "God has a way of growing people up, doesn't He?"

"Yes, He does."

Her voice was soft and so tender he shoved his hands in his pockets to keep from embracing her. "And besides, if we stay underground you can let me have it with both barrels for sneaking off without you."

"I'll save the lambasting for later." She eyed him closely. "You really think there are answers at Meadowlands that will show us what happened to Tess?"

He nodded. "Their behavior confirms it. The stakes are clearly life or death if they're willing to abduct me and—"

"And what? Kill you? Leave you to die? Is that why they dumped you here?"

"They couldn't exactly let me walk away." They both felt the chill of it. They were locked in with men who would have no problem killing to keep their secrets.

"Do you think Tess is alive?" she said quietly, handing him a flashlight while she activated a small lantern from her pack.

"I don't know but I'm going to find out."

"No working phone for me and I assume they've taken yours."

"Yes."

"So we've got only the supplies I have with me and a short window before they discover I've pried the lock off the tunnel door or see me in action on a video feed."

"That about sums it up."

"At least we're clear on the situation. Are you okay to travel?"

"No sweat." He tried his best not to let her see that his head was ringing like a gong and his legs felt like rubber. He covered by massaging Arthur's ears. "Thanks for finding me, old sport." He shot a glance at Beth. "You too, P."

She didn't scold him for the nickname. Instead she smiled. It cheered him. All was not lost. Yet. Was it even possible that they'd find a way back to some sort of relationship amidst these do-or-die circumstances?

When she cinched her pack, he held out his hands. "I can carry it."

"No, thanks. I got it."

He frowned. "All right. At least let me have the pup."

"That I'll go for. He's been tickling me with all his shenanigans." She extracted Poe from her makeshift carrier.

Poe was delighted to see him, darting that sliver of a tongue over his cheeks. "Come on, puppers. Get serious. There's a mission afoot."

"Keep him warm," Beth said. "He's still very weak."

"Yes, ma'am. You heard what your mama said." He stowed the dog inside his jacket, but let him stick his head out, raising the zipper all the way to Poe's chin.

They made a strange entourage, light bobbing as they glided through the underground gullet. Arthur trundled along. Poe jutted from Jack's clothing like a miniature figurehead on the prow of a ship. Jack took the lead, mindful of low beams and his forehead and she walked behind him. Their pace was slow since they had to wind their way through labyrinthian stacks of cardboard cartons and dust-covered supplies.

Beth peered close at a stack of boxes. "They're labeled Records." She opened the lid of the nearest one and pulled out a stack of paper. "Ledgers," she said. "Recent, from November of last year." She returned it and replaced the lid. "Real odd place to keep the books, isn't it?"

"Exactly what I was thinking."

"You suppose there is another set in the office for the accountant? The ones Daniel hired Tess to go over?"

He grimaced. "That's not a good thought, but probable. Most accounting tasks are done with software these days."

They pressed on for another hour, traversing areas that did not look as though they'd been disturbed for years. It was slow going since they had to climb around untidily stacked debris and relics from the park's history: old signs, fiber-glass decorations, messy coils of string bulbs.

They approached the entrance to a darker corridor, cramped with a lower ceiling, the sides piled with stacks of empty cardboard cartons, planks and buckets of small stakes. They eased through a creaking wood door.

"This place is a tinderbox, isn't it?" she said.

"Trying not to think about that right now."

Poe squirmed against his chest and whined, button nose quivering. "Let's stop a minute. Little buddy needs to stretch." He rooted in his jacket. "Okay, let me give you a…"

But as soon as he put Poe down on the floor, the dog hopped on his three good legs, tumbling, recovering, until he'd scurried to a pile of battered cardboard cartons. He stopped and his whine turned into a bloodcurdling howl. Arthur joined him, the hair on his scruff stiffening.

Poe let out a peal of high-pitched barking, just as the pile began to move.

SEVEN

Beth snatched up Poe to keep him from advancing. Jack pulled his fist back, ready for action. Whatever it was lying under the debris was much bigger than an animal, but in the meager light she couldn't make it out. Poe went wild against Beth's restraint. Arthur pawed to reach him, dividing his attention between Poe and the writhing pile. Jack moved forward, kicking aside the crumpled boxes. Now in view was a blue tarp, dirty and streaked with grease, and there was clearly someone underneath. He grasped a corner and swept it aside.

Beth gasped. Poe's howls increased.

A woman lay on her back, curly hair matted and tangled, dark eyes huge with terror. She jackknifed into a sitting position and crabwalked until she came to an abrupt stop. One of her ankles was chained to a metal ring affixed to the floor.

Chained. Beth felt sick. Treatment unacceptable for an animal, let alone a woman. Was this Tess? Could it be? She looked to be in her midthirties. Dark hair, like in the photo on Jack's phone, but the lighting was bad and the woman's face was partially obscured with smudges of dirt. It was early Friday morning. How long had she been imprisoned?

"We're not here to…" Jack started, but fear shone in the

woman's face as she strained against the chain in a futile attempt to distance herself farther from him.

Jack looked at Beth in mute uncertainty.

"Let me," Beth said, urging Jack to move a few paces away and handing him the wriggling Poe. She waited for the woman to go still before she came an inch or two forward.

"I'm Beth Wolfe. This is my bloodhound, Arthur. He's super gentle and he's very well-mannered."

She took them both in, her body taut as wire, breathing hard through her nose.

Beth eased a fraction closer and stroked Arthur to demonstrate. "Do you like dogs? Arthur adores people. He'd love to meet you, if that's okay."

When the woman did not try to jerk away, Beth spoke softly. "Arthur, meet and greet."

Arthur plopped to the floor and belly-crawled forward to present the crown of his head to the woman. It was a behavior they'd used repeatedly when dealing with a frightened child or confused elderly person. Bloodhounds were imposingly large, but this move made him appear smaller, less threatening. As per his training, Arthur moved at a snail's pace, gradually scooting closer, a few inches each moment, until his paw rested lightly on the woman's shin. Her whole body was trembling, but she watched Arthur without recoiling, her breath coming in deep gusts. More calm. Less panic. Good progress.

"It's going to be all right," Beth said brightly, kneeling next to her. "Arthur is a search dog. We're here to help you."

She was shivering mightily. Beth stripped off her Security Hounds jacket. "If it's okay, I'll put this around your shoulders while we figure out how to get your foot loose. Would that be all right?"

When tears leaked out of her eyes and she nodded, Arthur

scooted until he was lying across her legs, and laid his head on her lap, his warm ears draping like a blanket.

"Arthur will stay with you, how's that? He's the world's sweetest dog. A little slobbery and musky sometimes, but he'd never hurt a fly. He doesn't even chase squirrels or cats."

The woman didn't respond, but Beth thought her breathing was becoming more regular.

"Let me…" When Jack stepped close to help, the woman surged back again, so he froze. "I'm sorry. I didn't mean to scare you."

He stepped away while Beth tucked the jacket more firmly over her shoulders. "This will feel good. You're so cold from lying on this cement floor, aren't you?"

Arthur's warmth had to be pleasing in this dank place and the woman's hands stroked his neck, tears streaming down her face. Her lips were parched and cracked. "Yes."

"I'm sure you're thirsty."

Jack kept his distance, but whipped a water bottle from Beth's pack and uncapped it. Beth extended it. The woman grabbed it with both hands and gulped, water splashing down her chin, drinking until half the bottle was empty. Poe could not keep quiet and let out a plaintive warbling howl that echoed through the space.

The woman coughed and stared at Poe. "Is that…?" Her voice was rough and hoarse as if she'd been yelling for help. For how long, Beth wondered?

She glugged more water before continuing. "I was trying to help that dog, earn his trust with food treats until I could catch him."

She'd been trying to help Poe. Confirmation.

"You took a selfie with him, didn't you?"

The woman stared. "Yes. How did you know that?"

Nerves zinging, Beth nodded to Jack, who gingerly placed the dog near enough for the woman to snatch him up and cuddle him under her chin.

"I almost didn't recognize you in your Valentine sweater and all cleaned up," she whispered, kissing Poe. Arthur snuck in some licks for both of them. "I left food and water for you. I'm so glad you're okay."

"What's your name?" Beth said, over the pounding of her heart.

"Tess Altman."

Tess. Beth felt lightheaded. She heard Jack's quick inhale as he sank to a knee. Somehow she kept her voice calm and level. "Tess, this man behind me is Jack St. James." There was a flicker of interest in Tess's eyes. Did she recognize his name?

Jack smiled. "Pleased to meet you."

Beth swallowed. "His son...our son, contacted him to find you."

"You're... Adam's parents?" The question came out no louder than a whisper.

Beth could hardly get the words out. "His birth parents, yes."

Tess looked from one to the other. "Adam told me about you, Mr. St. James."

But not Beth, of course, the mother he'd never met, who'd not shown any interest. She swallowed hard.

"Please call me Jack."

"Adam asked you to find me?"

Jack nodded. "Yes, he called me Monday and said you'd stopped communicating with him a couple days before."

"What day is it now?"

"Very early Friday."

She gaped. "I've been down here for seven days."

Beth's brain reeled. How was the woman still alive?

Jack exchanged a look with Beth. "I was trying to find some clue that would tell me what had become of you, but I got caught by the security guard and dumped in here." He winked at Beth. "But this cagey lady and her dog rescued me and then we found you."

Tess closed her eyes. "It's all like a nightmare. I can't believe it."

Jack began to comb through the stacked debris. "Keep talking, okay? I'll listen while I work on how to get you free."

"So it's true then," Beth said. "You're...Adam's girl-friend?"

She nodded and her expression softened. "We met at a coffee shop in Southern California where I was staked out at a table working on spreadsheets." She smiled. "We've been seeing each other for six months now. I love him so much. We were going to be married when I finished my contract here and he got back from his overseas assignment."

Her son and his fiancée. Beth had dreamed so often about Adam's circumstances, wondered if he'd found someone to love, if he'd gotten married. And in this horrible tunnel she'd come face-to-face with the answers. It felt as if God had sealed up a wound in that moment, an invisible wound, here in this dank place. Her heart beat a little stronger.

Tess paused. "I didn't know he'd met his birth mother too."

"Uh, he hasn't. I mean, we haven't." Beth fought for control. *Not yet.*

Poe wriggled closer and Tess laughed and kissed him. "You remember me, don't you, sweetie?"

"He sure does," Jack said over his shoulder. "He alerted

us that you were under the tarp. Otherwise we might have walked right on by. We named him Poe, short for Napoleon."

"I like it." Tess caressed the dog, who laid his tiny head on her shoulder, the picture of contentment.

Tess groaned. "Adam must have been so worried when I didn't reply."

"How have you survived this long without food and water?"

"I had a couple of protein bars in my fanny pack. They dumped that here with me after they took my phone." She shook her head. "But would you believe one of these boxes contained some ancient cotton candy and soda bottles? It's all stale and crusty but it's been my breakfast and dinner."

"Good sugar source. You're really clever to forage like that," Jack said.

"Amazing what you'll do to stay alive. If I get out of here I'm never eating cotton candy or drinking soda pop ever again." Her brows knit. "They probably think I've died of dehydration by now."

Beth tamped down her disgust that anyone could inflict such suffering. Best to confirm the facts. "We need to know exactly who took you here and why. Can you tell us?"

Jack continued to shine his light on the chains, but she knew he was hanging on every word like she was.

Tess shook the wild hair from her face, which set Poe to licking her chin again. "I didn't see who struck me down and I don't know all of the 'why,' but I think Ray and Wyatt Cumberland were stealing money from the park. Their elder brother, Daniel, was the one who hired me to audit the books. The numbers they gave me just didn't match up so I had to dig deeper, look into bank records. I'd just started to download more comprehensive documents when this happened."

"You were working for Daniel?"

"Yes, he's the one who made contact, but he told me it was a joint decision by the three brothers to have an audit. Wyatt and Ray seemed reluctant to have me around, though. They were confused when I showed up the first day and asked them for documents and access—either that or they were pretending to be. I had Zoom chats with Daniel and he praised my stick-to-itiveness so that kept me going. He travels for a tech company, but he checked in regularly. I told him I was finding inconsistencies and he arranged a meeting with all three brothers and me. It was supposed to take place..." She paused. "This Friday night. A week ago, I was in the office downloading information stored on the server. I heard Ray talking to Wyatt on the phone. Wyatt had flown out of town on some business and I got this frightening feeling that they meant to get rid of me. You know what they say about a woman listening to her instincts. I waited until they left and quietly gathered up my stuff and hurried to the parking lot. I felt like I had to get out of there and call the police, but someone grabbed me from behind and choked me until I passed out. I woke up here without my phone or my computer."

Beth patted her cold hand when the tears started again. "I'm so sorry."

"I'm sure Ray saw me sneaking off and decided to make me disappear or told Bud to do it. They left me to die and I would have if you hadn't found me."

Jack turned from his examination of the concrete. "I remember now. Adam called me, worried why you'd gone silent." Jack's voice lifted in excitement. "He said no one at the park had any answer as to where you'd gone, only that you quit abruptly. He called the cops and they found no sign that you'd been harmed. They said it was too early to file a missing person's report. After that, the brothers stopped taking Adam's calls and he became really worried."

"What about Daniel?" Her mouth trembled. "He was good to me. He took a big risk hiring me and exposing them. Do you know what happened to him?"

"No," Jack said. "We haven't been able to reach him."

Tess's gaze swept the tunnel. "He's probably down here somewhere too."

"We'll find him if we can, okay?" Beth urged her to drink more water.

Tess frowned. "All I know is Ray and Wyatt were siphoning money without Daniel's knowledge. It was pretty clear they'd given me a dummy set of books and obviously they'd do anything to avoid jail."

Including murder.

"Wait a minute. Something they said when I snuck into the park. They said, 'We can get it on our way out of town.'"

"There's a cash account. They'll withdraw the money." Tess stroked Poe as she considered. "It's not a bunch, but they can take up to $100,000 without requiring Daniel's signature, as long as they have the two brothers to authorize."

"And Daniel's gone silent," Jack said.

"Then why the urgency for them to leave if they've already murdered him?" Jack said.

"Maybe they're concerned about getting away before he's reported missing by his coworkers at the tech company," Tess said.

She and Jack exchanged a look of agreement. There could very well be a third victim dumped somewhere in the dark tunnels besides Jack and Tess. There was no time to commit to a search for Daniel without a scent article. Tess looked pale and wan, her cheekbones prominent, body weak. It remained to be seen if she would be able to walk.

Jack tugged experimentally on the chain where it joined the iron ring. "It's pretty solid, but right here at the bolt the cement is cracked. If I could find something heavy to bash it with…" He went foraging in the shadows. Beth found a granola bar for Tess.

She ate hungrily. Poe licked the crumbs from her mouth. She broke off a little bit for him, which he whisked off the tip of her finger. If Beth had any doubts before, her spirit was put at ease. She knew in that instant what kind of person Tess Altman was. Near starving, she'd share with her faithful friend, Poe.

Beth blinked back tears. *You picked a good one, Adam.* And she said a prayer that God would give her the opportunity and the courage to tell him so someday.

"Well, now, what have we here? Come to Papa," Jack enthused as he extracted a crowbar from beneath a wrecked pallet "This should do the trick."

Tess's eyes lit with hope.

"I'll close the door to muffle the noise."

"Lock it too," Jack said. "Just for good measure."

Beth took Poe and set him with Arthur, away from any flying debris. Poe tried to escape but Arthur clamped him down gently with a paw to keep him in place in spite of his indignant bark. She held up an emergency blanket from her supplies to shield herself and Tess as Jack attacked the cement, flaking away the stone a chip at a time. The sound no doubt traveled, but there was nothing they could do about that. He'd worked up a sweat and she knew it had to be agonizing with his recent battering, but he slammed the crowbar at a frenzied pace. With one final massive whack, she heard the bolt snap off and the chain slither free.

"That's what I'm talkin' about," Jack crowed.

Beth dropped the blanket and high-fived his upturned

palm. She knelt at Tess's feet. Though Tess was freed from the wall, the shackle and the chain soldered onto it were still attached to her ankle. It would be heavy going and noisy to haul it with them in their escape.

"Now that we've got the extra slack, do you think we can get your foot free?" Beth pulled off Tess's shoe and peeled away the sock. Her ankle was bruised and raw from the hours she'd spent trying to escape, but with the new maneuverability and Beth's help, inch by inch she squeezed the rusted cuff over her foot.

When it clanked to the floor, Tess clasped her hands together and prayed. "Thank you, God. Thank you."

Heart brimming, Beth embraced her and they cried together for a moment in their gratitude. *Freedom.* She added her own tearful thanks.

As she applied a dressing and bandage to Tess's ravaged ankle, her mind moved to the next steps. The escape was temporary, along with their safety. They were still trapped in an amusement park with murderous men.

Jack's expression told her he was thinking that too. If they didn't get moving, the brothers or Bud would find them. Soon.

Jack forced away the anger and frustration. If he hadn't been delayed by the attack at Java Jake's and his memory loss, hadn't waited to sneak into the park, hadn't let Bud get the drop on him, he might have arrived sooner, avoided capture, found the answers in the office and freed Tess from needless suffering.

But the chances that he'd have escaped his bonds and actually located Tess by himself? Without Beth and the dogs? Zilch.

So God had delivered him to the very place he needed

with the resources he required to save his own life and Tess's. God had provided Beth. It felt so natural to be with her again, working on a shared goal, her energy and courage brighter than he'd ever seen it. And if he admitted it, the attraction he'd always felt for her had flamed into something different, but no less compelling.

And now they'd both met the woman Adam loved. God's ways were mysterious indeed.

Beth settled a knit cap over Tess's mop of hair before she pulled on a spare windbreaker herself. He wished Beth would put on a knit cap too, since it was frigid, but he suspected she only had one.

They helped Tess to her feet, catching her when her knees buckled. "I need a little rest, that's all. I'll be okay in a minute."

But her breathing was shallow and fast, and her skin looked clammy. Beth didn't voice concern, but he could read it in her expression. Seven days with minimal food in a freezing cement tomb had taken their toll.

They found her a dry place to sit and deposited the whining Poe in her lap.

"You transport the little guy, okay?" Jack figured it would both give her something to focus on and allow him free hands in case of attack.

He felt the burning urgency to move in spite of Tess's condition, the sense there was a target on their backs in neon paint. "I can carry you, Tess." With the low ceilings and debris strewn everywhere, it would be hazardous. More hazardous than delaying their escape? Unlikely.

"Five minutes," Beth commanded, giving Tess another bottle of water. "I'd like her to hydrate more before we push on." He deciphered her not-so-subtle message. Tess wasn't

well and what lay ahead might tax her more than her depleted body could handle.

Arthur swiveled his head.

"Whatcha got, boy?" Jack asked.

"He's—" Beth broke off as they both heard it now.

"What?" Tess whispered.

The door cracked as someone kicked it, splintering a hole
in the wood. The heel of a boot came through. He heard Bud
swearing as he freed himself and reached through the gap,
meaty fingers grasping for the lock.

"I don't know how you did it, but it's not gonna help,"
Bud shouted. "You're delaying the inevitable, St. James."

Tess crumpled in fear but Beth wedged a shoulder under
her armpit and he hurried to support her other side. They
rushed her away and into the next room where Jack slammed
the door behind them, throwing the latch.

It wasn't strong and it wouldn't keep Bud out for long. He
dragged over a heavy crate and shoved it against the wood.

"Best we can do for now," he said. "Gotta move fast."

The minutes stretched in agonizing slowness as they hurried their way along. It was a race for survival now and the
slow moving party of three humans and two dogs had hardly
left the starting blocks.

They continued on as fast as they could until Tess sagged
between them. Her legs were clearly shaky and her stamina
would not last.

"I'm sorry," she said. "My body won't seem to cooper-
ate no matter how much I try."

"It's okay." Beth's expression told a different story. Bud
would catch up any minute.

"How about this?" He went to Tess, draped her arm
around his shoulders. "Just the two of us, like those three
legged races, right?"

Her face was lined with fatigue and pain, but she gave him a firm nod. "That will be perfect. I can do it."

She had grit. Like Beth. A tiny gold cross glimmered at her throat. Adam had picked himself a winner.

And you did too, once upon a time. Too bad they hadn't been grown-up enough to see what was at stake.

Beth secured Poe in Tess's pocket and repositioned her backpack.

Arthur slung his head around, ears swinging like pendulums. Poe craned his neck from his cloth pouch a moment later and cocked his miniature ears.

"They hear something," Beth whispered. Tess's fingers clutched his shoulder.

Seconds later the door was under assault. "He's going to break through the barricade," Tess whispered.

Jack craned his neck and caught a glimpse. The wood trembled but held; flakes drifted off into the dank air.

The next few kicks and it would give way.

"I'll make it harder."

"No," Beth snapped. "We have to run."

He ignored her because there really was no place to run. The only way was to play for time. He let go of Tess, who leaned on Beth, and ran back and shoved another pile of boxes against the door.

He returned to the women. "That will give us a few more minutes before he breaks through."

Tess was shaking, her face waxy in the dark. "They'll kill me. They won't let us get away."

He took hold of her again. "No one is going to hurt you, Tess. I won't let them and neither will Beth."

Tess bit her cracked lip.

He nodded to Beth and she burst into motion. By the aid of her small light, she and Arthur led the way to the exit door. There was no lock so they closed it and he wedged a piece of wood under the jamb. The door led into yet another dark and cluttered passageway. He moved clumsily after her, supporting Tess.

Maybe he could find something in the way of a weapon as they fled. A hammer? A sturdy board? Anything would do. He wished he'd carried along the crowbar. Bud was not going to have a chance to deploy his Taser again, if Jack had a say in the matter. Had he an additional weapon? Did the brothers? No telling.

They lurched along, trying to find a coordinating rhythm. Each step seemed to cause Tess pain so he tried to take more of the weight off her mangled ankle.

Behind him, the creak of breaking wood, more shouts and obscenities.

Tess gulped back a scream.

He didn't let her look, but propelled them both, following Beth and the dogs. They hurtled through two passageways that seemed to plunge them deeper into the ground. He stopped long enough at each juncture to jam the door shut as he had before. His plan was working to some degree because the sound of pursuit was fainter now as Bud had to stop to force his way through the obstacles.

They burst into another narrow room, which housed all kinds of machinery, blackened with age. Wooden pallets stacked waist-high with bundled newspapers created a maze of hurdles. The ceiling was open in places, covered by barred utility screens that allowed him to see through to the underpinnings of the rollercoaster. They were beneath the belly of the beast.

Tess was breathing hard, in obvious pain. "Rest for a minute?"

He perched her on a newspaper pile.

Beth gave Arthur and Poe a quick drink and urged a water bottle on Tess.

Jack surveyed the stacks, trying to work out the point of what he was seeing. Beth wasn't long in giving voice to his question.

"Newspapers," she said as she shone her light around the bundles. "Hundreds of them. Why would they store newspapers down here?"

Exactly what puzzled him as well. He checked the nearest front page. "This is last week's edition. Added recently then."

A room full of dry newspapers. That set off a drumbeat of anxiety in his gut that made the delay even more difficult. A fire would be the perfect means to conceal bodies. Is that how they'd meant to dispose of Tess, perhaps Daniel also? But there would be a thorough examination of this underground space, especially with a wildfire sweeping through the area. Perhaps that approaching disaster had sparked a deadly idea, buying the brothers enough time for them to empty the bank account and leave before Daniel arrived. Had big brother foiled their plans and they'd killed him?

Why bother burning the place, though, if they were going to bolt anyway?

More questions than answers.

His brain fixed on another topic that he could no longer ignore. They were being pursued by one man minimum. Bud. If it were Jack, he'd have split up the team, made sure the eggs weren't all in one basket, sent Ray and Wyatt to other positions. There were only a few exits to cover and he'd have assigned them to circle around if the prey tried to exit.

Beth was eyeing him closely. "Plan change?" She could read him like a book, even after all these years.

"If Bud has any smarts, he's alerted Ray and Wyatt to our location and they'll have someone waiting at the exit. Or flush us out like rabbits."

She nodded. "I was thinking that too. So what's your idea?"

He looked up at the roller coaster, visible through the grates only five feet above them. Hazy moonlight trickled through the screens. It was going on 3 a.m. Only a few more hours before sunrise. "How do you feel about roller coasters?"

Beth considered. "You know I love them under better circumstances. Unpredictability is our only option, since we're likely trapped on both ends. If we can exit where they don't expect us, we might buy more time." She gazed thoughtfully up into the moonlight. "The climbing up there part I'm not too sure about."

Jack was mentally calculating. "We can stack the paper bundles into a rough staircase that will bring us close enough. I'll carry Tess up, then help you and the dogs up onto the platform."

Tess wrapped her arms around herself. "What about the cameras? They'll see us as soon as we pop out."

"Maybe not. The cameras are for the public areas. They won't cover the base of the roller coaster and there's a lot of steel structure and wood supports for concealment. We can make our way along, find a place with an emergency phone that works, possibly. If not, we continue on toward the rear like we'd planned. Climb out. Get help." He tried to infuse his words with confidence, but the women were no fools. They both understood they were in a dire predicament.

Tess folded her arms and sniffed. Arthur went to her, dripping water from his snout on her torn jeans and Poe burrowed under her chin. "You should go without me. I can't keep up."

Fat chance. "Lovely gesture. Not an option," Jack said cheerfully.

Tess shook her head. "They'll catch us if you try and lug me along. I slow us down. That's the truth and we all know that."

Beth started to speak, but Jack bent and put a hand on Tess's shoulder. "Listen to me, Tess. There is not one tiny shred of possibility that I'm leaving you down here by yourself. Beth agrees, I can tell."

"Absolutely," Beth said.

"It's settled then. We're going, all of us, together, and I don't want to hear another word about it. Am I clear?"

She nodded, not quite looking at him. "Yes. Thank you."

"All right, then." When he straightened, he realized Beth was staring at him in a way he hadn't seen before. Her eyes were soft, head cocked slightly as if she was considering him in a new way.

He wanted to tell her, *I'm not the young man you knew.* As much as he wished he had his twenty-year-old body sometimes, he wouldn't trade what he'd learned, how he'd grown and matured, how he'd learned to trust in God.

And she wasn't the same Beth he'd known back then either; that was clear too. Just as wonderful, but in a grown-up way. The Lord had effected good in both of their lives.

He smiled and she smiled back.

"Ready to blow this popsicle stand, P.?"

Her laugh lit a spark to his determination.

"Yes, Jack. Let's do this."

EIGHT

Beth helped Jack drag the heavy stacks of newspapers into a sort of ungainly staircase. One layer, then two, and a third that would deliver them within a few feet of the metal grating. She crawled up and removed the screws from the fasteners with a Phillips screwdriver from her pack.

It was an awkward and lengthy process since she had to stick her arm through the grating and unscrew them from the topside. Jack tried, but his arms were too big to fit. When she accomplished the mission, he scrambled to help her shove the heavy coverings aside. Shoulder to shoulder, a unified team.

That's what she'd thought they were back in the day. Young kids who could weather any storm life threw at them, relying on their own dubious strength instead of God's. When she touched him, she remembered all the mistakes she wanted to forget. So why then did part of her long to keep him close? The whole situation was beyond strange.

"Remind me to bring you along to the next occasion when I'm imprisoned." His admiring grin was pleasing. Too pleasing. Simply the kind of rapport people develop when they're in survival mode. Trauma bonding. That had to be the explanation.

Trauma was nothing new for her and Jack. They'd experienced the upheaval of an unplanned pregnancy, a secret one they'd shared with no one, and then the release of their boy to be raised by strangers. Trauma indeed. But they hadn't bonded over it certainly, not then. More her choice than his. He'd tried, harder than she had, to maintain their connection. It simply hurt in a way that was unbearable. Her own grief would not allow her to seek healing with Jack or anyone else.

And whatever you're experiencing now isn't healing either, she told herself, pocketing the screws.

She inserted more space between them as they continued to shove aside the last obstruction, doing her best to keep the metal from clanging against the massive iron girders. When it finally came loose, they got a clear view of the underside of the roller coaster.

The smoky predawn was jarring after so many hours in complete darkness, but she welcomed it. She felt like a mole emerging from its den. She stuck her head out for a cautious look around. The beams jutted up like exposed bones.

"No sign of anyone," she reported, trying to ignore the feel of Jack's steadying grip on her forearm as she climbed back down. "We're at the center of the roller coaster where the incline leads up to the big drop." She smirked. "You know, the point where you'd start screaming like a preschooler if we were on the ride."

He arched his brow. "I wish it to be noted for the record that my voice is much manlier than a preschooler's."

"If you say so." She stifled a giggle as she pointed. "In that direction there's a service ladder we can climb down from the platform if the coast is clear."

Jack considered. "That should put us at the east side of the coaster, if I'm thinking straight."

"And then?" Tess asked.

She brushed the dust off her jeans. "Like Jack said, we search for a phone or a place where I get reception on my cell while we make for the nearest spot to breach the fence."

Tess nodded. "Cell reception is terrible in the park. Wi-Fi too. I couldn't get anything unless I was in the office."

"That might be another option. Get a call out."

Tess brightened and extracted something from her fanny pack. "I can bring something to the escape party," she said. "It's the office key. My attackers didn't bother to take it."

Jack grinned and pocketed it. "Many thanks, Tess, since my lock-picking skills are poor. We could even barricade ourselves in the office or make a run for it, if that presents itself sooner."

Tess looked dubious. "Run for it?"

Beth sighed. "They've undoubtedly already found our vehicles, maybe moved or disabled them."

Tess stroked Poe. "I don't know what they did with my car. I worked so hard to pay it off."

"Probably hidden somewhere because the cops didn't report they'd found it. That would have put them on higher alert."

Jack turned to Beth. "There was a barricade closing off the northbound highway when I drove in. Still there when you arrived?"

Beth nodded. "There may be some personnel there monitoring. It's only about six miles." Six miles would be easy for her and Jack, and even Arthur if she rested him, but Tess wasn't in any shape for a hike.

"Options. Excellent." Jack's tone was light, but she wasn't fooled. They were in trouble.

A low thud vibrated the floor and sent Arthur's ears flapping. Their pursuer, closing in. Jack had already jammed a wooden shim under the door to slow their access but it wouldn't hold for long. "We need to go."

Jack nodded. "Tess, a piggyback ride would be the easiest way to get you out of here if you can hang on to me."

"I can."

Beth took Poe from Tess and helped her onto the first tier of newspapers. Jack crouched enough so that she could climb onto his back and wrap her arms around his shoulders. She was clearly weak.

Just a little while longer, Tess. You can do it.

Jack stood and started up the makeshift steps. Beth scaled up after them to prevent Tess from falling too far if she let go.

From below, Poe whined in confusion, but when he hopped away, Arthur patiently gathered him close again.

After a few heart-stopping moments, Beth watched Jack and Tess approach the opening. From somewhere deep in the tunnel came a dull whack as another of Jack's makeshift barricades fell. She silently urged him to move faster, but it was a painful effort to haul them both out. She breathed easier when they cleared the grate, vanishing for a moment to set down his burden.

When he popped his head back over the edge of the grate and looked down at her, he was winded, dripping with sweat, but triumphant. "Okay. Part one, accomplished. Now you climb up. Bring Poe if you can. I'll go back down and carry Arthur, if that's okay with you."

She didn't want to agree. Arthur was her partner and her responsibility. It pained her to admit that she would be hard pressed to carry her 120-pound bloodhound with her back newly healed from surgery. Had her sons and sons-in-law been present, they would have jumped into action without consulting her. Jack in his youth would have done the same. Now he was asking.

Nice, she thought, nodding up at him. She tucked Poe in her front pocket and gave Arthur a caress. "You know I won't leave you here, baby. You'll only be alone for a minute or two, promise. We'll have you out of here in a jiffy, okay?" She left the small lantern next to him, activated so he wouldn't be alone in the dark. Probably silly, since he had much better night vision than she did, but it helped her soul.

Arthur wagged his tail and maintained his sit while she clambered up, uncomfortable at leaving her dog. At the top of the newspaper steps, Jack took her arm and helped her hoist herself out.

"Going for Arthur."

"His back legs…" She stopped. "I mean, he has arthritis in his rear paws."

Jack touched her hair, his fingers trailing warmth. "I know he's your baby, P. I will be as gentle as I possibly can."

She felt a sudden lump in her throat. "Thank you."

"My privilege." Jack lowered himself into the tunnel again.

His privilege? To help her and her dog? After years of silence between them? She crawled on hands and knees across the metal panels to where Tess was crouched next to an enormous girder. The sky was not yet showing signs of morning. The platform felt cold, as if she was crawling over a sheet of ice. The scent of smoke was stronger now.

Beth handed Poe over and pressed her palm to Tess's brow. "You okay?"

She nodded, but now with the help of the meager light, Beth could see she was far from it. A slender woman to begin with, her cheekbones were prominent in her gaunt face, her limbs trembled badly and her breathing was rapid and shallow. Beth didn't like the dullness in her eyes and the warmth of her forehead that could indicate a fever. As soon as they got to a more secure location, she would take a quick temperature. There wasn't too much she could offer if Tess was fighting an infection except ibuprofen to bring the fever down and help her feel better. Buying time, that's all they could do. She felt Tess looking at her closely.

"Sorry. I didn't mean to stare, but Adam has your eyes and Jack's hair."

Beth felt simultaneous twinges of joy and sorrow. She wasn't sure what to say but she hungered to hear even the tiniest detail about the son she'd never met. "I, um, Jack says he's a good man."

"He is. The best." Her smile was dreamy. "So, you and Jack aren't together anymore?"

The question startled her. "Uh, no. This is the first time I've seen him since we gave Adam to the adoption agency."

Tess's eyes flew wide. "I'm surprised. You work together like a couple."

A couple? Beth blushed. "Emergency situation, that's all."

"That's too bad that you split up. It would be such a hard thing to do. I know a couple who made the same choice to give up their baby and they really bonded over it."

"We didn't." The words came out harsh and clipped. Why hadn't they bonded over their grief? Because of a million reasons and mistakes, mostly hers.

"I'm sorry, Mrs. Wolfe. I was butting in where I don't belong."

"Please call me Beth and no apology necessary." Tess looked tentative, so Beth gave her a squeeze. "Truly. I'm going to help Jack with Arthur. Okay?"

She offered a rueful grin. "Adam says my curiosity will get me in trouble someday." Her mouth trembled as she looked around. "I guess he was right. I should have run when I first met Ray and Wyatt. I knew they were hiding something."

"You couldn't know," Beth said. "It's all right."

She left Tess cradling Poe and crept back to the opening, pain still circling inside. Her boy was a combination of both of them.

I know a couple who made the same choice and they really bonded over it. Water under the bridge, but she felt the ache of it. She and Jack could have been friends, at least, if she wasn't so fragile. A friend didn't fill the same space as a child or spouse, but that had been too much, more than her tattered heart could take. Still, she and Jack had an undeniable tether between them—their son, Adam, who had her blue eyes and Jack's unruly dark hair.

She focused on Jack as he appeared over the opening, Arthur draped around his shoulders. The knot in her stomach unclenched at the sight of her beloved bloodhound. As soon as Jack cleared enough, she grabbed his arm and helped him scramble out. He knelt and she assisted Arthur to get free. The dog gave himself a mighty shake after the stressful event, and slathered Beth with a sloppy kiss before he gave one to Jack as well.

She stroked Arthur's saggy face. On impulse, she kissed Jack on his stubbly cheek. "Thank you, not just for toting Arthur, but…for reaching out to Adam."

"Still angry that I didn't tell you?"

"A little."

"But you'll get over it?" His grin was infectious.

"Let's see if we survive this. Then we'll talk."

"Don't think I'll forget it, P."

He wouldn't forget it? What? The fragile connection

they'd somehow built? She shied away from the idea. Too scary. Too many risks.

But if God was offering her a way to heal with her son and Jack? She wouldn't forget it either.

Friendship, she told herself.

That would be enough.

Jack kept the group moving, climbing over beams and around massive anchors buried deep in the thick cement slab. He kept a close eye on Arthur whom he desperately hoped would alert them if he sensed someone approaching. He and Beth had to practically lift Tess over and around the obstacles as her strength waned. Finally they reached the edge where the metal ladder would lead them down off the cement platform and return them to the amusement park grounds. To their deaths?

He gestured for them to stop. Beth handed him her binoculars and he scanned. Motion from the extreme far side of the park caught his attention. He zoomed in and held his tongue against the frustration that wanted to spew out.

"What is it?" Beth whispered.

He sank down on his haunches to report. "I can see one of the trailers where the brothers live. There's someone inside. I can see them moving around in there but I can't make a positive ID. I'd hazard a guess it's Ray."

"What does that mean?" Tess said.

"It means we can't get to the rear exits without being spotted by whoever is in the trailers," Beth explained. "No way out."

"Not at the moment." There might be a chance to arrange a diversion. He filed that away for future reference. "So the next option is the office. Tap into the Wi-Fi and make a call for help. Hopefully Bud will be struggling through our barricades and we know at least one brother is in the trailer."

"That still leaves another one unaccounted for."

"We'll deal with him if we have to." He gestured to his shoulders. "Another piggyback ride?"

"How can you? You must be exhausted," Tess said.

"Looking forward to a corn dog later. Gotta burn off the calories." His joke worked and she smiled. Beth helped Tess onto his back and he climbed down. Then Beth made the journey with Poe and he returned to carry Arthur again.

"This is getting to be a habit." He struggled to get the dog on his shoulders. Arthur slobbered all over him until they reached the bottom rung of the ladder, when Jack could wipe his face. "Bloodhound drool is no small thing."

"You got that right."

On ground level, they took a moment to reconnoiter. The office was due east along a trail marked Service Vehicles Only. Though the way was shrouded in smoke and clusters of trees, he was certain of the direction.

"How far?"

"Not very." It was all relative, he figured. Better for her not to know it was a good quarter mile as the crow flew.

They supported her between them, the minutes passing into half hours and beyond. They had to stop so often for Tess to rest it felt as though they were moving in slow motion. Finally Tess lost all strength and he carried her on his back, his own body quivering with the effort. The hazy sun was visible when they emerged near a paved trail and collapsed in the shelter of a snack shack.

"We're almost there. I can barely see the office from here."

"Rest," Tess panted. "Just for a moment."

Smoke coiled through the air and Beth coughed.

They had to obtain shelter, at least temporarily. He tried the front door, which was bolted, naturally. The windows were covered in metal slats. Around the side was another door, also locked, with an old-fashioned padlock and metal latch.

Beth eyed the setup as she hustled over to him. "We've got to get her out of this wind for a few minutes. She's so cold."

He was too, his toes numbing. "Normally I'd be against breaking and entering, but things being what they are…"

"Exactly. I don't know how to pick locks. This way's faster." She stepped past him, the small pry tool in her hand. "I'm getting to be a regular burglar." She pried off the metal hinge and the padlock fell away.

He helped Tess and they bundled inside. He pulled the door closed and made sure Tess was propped against the wall. With the shutters pried open a half inch, they gained some illumination but still prevented anyone from seeing much inside. It was enough for them to examine their new quarters. The interior was small with a metal service counter and a minimal kitchen setup.

Tess sank to the floor with Poe on her lap. "Smells like grilled cheese sandwiches," she said after a sniff. "I bought one every day while I was here. Delicious and I always saved a corner for Poe. He's a cheese hound." She let Poe down to hop around and Beth supplied water in a bowl from which both dogs guzzled.

"One of God's finest foods." Jack's stomach growled. "Let's see what we can rustle up. The park closed abruptly so there must still be supplies. I figure Ray and his brother owe us lunch since they've sent Bud to kill us and all."

Beth stopped him. "I'll fix it," she said. "You rest."

He was too tired to argue. His legs felt like rubber bands.

The morning was rapidly passing. Though they were only a short distance from the office, at their pace it would take another half hour.

Come on, Jack. You're thinking like an old man.

He sat on the floor next to Tess, leaned his aching head back and let his legs recuperate until Beth returned, a glorious stack of sandwiches in her hands.

"We can't grill them, but there's plenty of bread and cheese and canned sodas. The water's running too so we can refill our bottles."

Absolute manna, he thought.

Before they started in, Tess offered to pray. Her voice faint and weak, she said a humble grace.

Beth's lips quivered and he felt his own eyes dampen as they said the amen. He added a silent plea that the Lord would help him get these two women, precious to him and Adam, out of the park alive along with their dogs. He'd known their son, had the ultimate blessing of meeting him, and now he desperately wanted Beth to have that experience too.

So much so that he'd risk everything to make it happen.

His pulse pounded as he looked at Beth, who cared for the dogs before herself, providing them food—Poe's from a blend she'd stowed in a plastic baggie. She insisted Tess take a dose of ibuprofen. How could he feel such a flood of emotion after they'd only been reconnected for two days? He realized he was staring at her and turned his attention to his sandwich and took a huge bite. "Honestly the best ungrilled sandwich I've ever eaten in my natural-born life. The chef should earn three Michelin Stars."

Beth laughed and offered a piece of cheese to each dog. "I'll put that on my résumé."

Arthur took his dessert delicately and began to lick it

with his massive tongue. Poe gobbled his with such fervor little pieces went flying everywhere, which provided more entertainment for him and giggles from Tess.

Tess only ate a mouthful in spite of Beth's urging. Her energy seemed to be almost gone.

Worrying.

While they ate, he checked Beth's phone on the off chance the snack shack would provide some sort of signal. It didn't. He ate a second sandwich and heaved himself to his feet. The view outside was quiet, gloomy. When he turned back Beth was kneeling next to Tess, whose eyes were closed. Beth's forehead was lined with concern.

"Tess?" When Beth patted Tess's shoulder, she didn't move. She spoke louder and Tess's eyes opened.

His relief left him weak.

"I'm sorry," Tess said and then her eyes closed.

Poe finished his crumb search and scrambled onto Tess's lap, pawing and whining to get a response.

Beth checked her vitals. "Can you hear me, Tess?"

Tess nodded slightly but kept her eyes shut. "I'm okay, I just can't move right now. So tired."

Beth took an emergency blanket from her pack and spread it over the young woman. Poe immediately burrowed under it and lay on her chest. Added warmth and comfort. The best medicine. But how long could she survive this way? Sick and hiding and on the run?

A tear leaked from Tess's closed eyes.

"It's all right, honey," Beth said, stroking her cheek. "You're doing great. Adam would be real proud. You rest for now."

Tess nodded slightly.

Beth and Jack moved to the far corner of the room.

"It's too much for her right now," she whispered.

And for him. As much as he wanted to, he couldn't carry Tess and look out for attack.

Beth's eyes met his. "You have to go to the office without us."

He opened his mouth to protest as he gazed at her lovely face, but there was no good argument to be made. She was right. They would have to separate. She pulled her phone from her pocket and gave it to him.

"Here," she said. "The first number in the address book is Garrett's. Soon as you can get a text to him, he'll start the rescue in motion. My kids will move mountains and they'll be here as soon as humanly possible with or without police support."

He clutched the phone. Just one small message could save them. The screen was locked. "Code?"

After a pause, she told him the numbers and his heart skipped. It was the birthdate of their son.

He smiled at her. "We're going to get through this and you'll meet him, P. You'll adore him."

Her lips trembled and he loved her for it.

"I always have," she whispered.

"And he's going to know that too. Soon."

She swallowed. "Did you...did you think I was a bad mother for insisting we give him away? Is that why you didn't tell me you'd decided to find him?"

He pressed her wrists. "No, P. Not at all. You were the best mother for Adam. You gave him everything you could. It had to be your choice to step into his life, not just a reaction because I did."

Her voice was hoarse with emotion. "He must hate me."

"He doesn't."

"But he must wonder why I never contacted him. What did you tell him about me?"

"That you are an amazing woman who made an excruciating choice so he could have a good life." He cleared his throat. "The right choice."

"I thought you disagreed."

"I did. And I held on to a lot of pain about that, but I finally understood you were right. I was a selfish kid at that point. I would have been a terrible father."

She pulled in a shaky breath and a tear leaked down her face, which he caught with his thumb. He lingered there, drinking her in, the fiery, headstrong teen who had grown into a magnificent woman. How easy it would be to fall in love with her all over again.

"Go," she said, pushing him away. "And don't get hurt, okay?"

He eased the door open and crept outside.

NINE

Beth held the door open just wide enough for Jack to squeeze out. Before he did, he kissed her on the cheek.

"We got this, P."

She surprised herself by kissing him back. "In it to win it," she said. Their favorite motto from back in the day when they happened to be getting along. Jack appeared delighted before he jogged off.

Before the door closed, Arthur stuck out his snout, sniffing madly, and shoved at her knee as if he would push through the door.

"Missing Jack already?" she said. *Me too.*

But Arthur tilted his head in that way that meant he'd glommed onto a scent he wanted to investigate. Something in the smoke-filled air had snagged his attention. "Not now, sweetie. That will have to wait."

When Jack got far enough away she closed the door and switched to the binoculars to track him until he vanished into the smoke.

Tess stirred and she went to her, readjusting the blanket. Arthur turned his attention to sniffing determinedly at Tess until Beth pushed him away. "Give her some space, Lovebug."

Tess sighed and when she roused a bit, Beth offered her

another sip of water and a bite of the sandwich she'd had to keep on the counter to protect it from Poe and Arthur.

"Thank you. I'll be better in a few minutes." She shivered. "It's so cold in here. What I wouldn't give for a hot bath."

"Oh, me too, preferably with bubbles."

Arthur nosed Tess again until she giggled. "I'm doing my best, dog. Pestering won't help."

"At least Poe is keeping you warm."

Tess embraced the little dog, who'd curled up into the dimensions of a cinnamon bun, the picture of contentment. She was tucking the blanket closer when Arthur cocked his head.

She and Tess locked eyes and froze as the purr of a motor grew louder.

Beth scurried to the shutters and peeked out.

Bud was approaching on the cart. Heart slamming, she eased the bolt shut as quietly as she could, closed the shutters fully, and gave Arthur the silent command. Tess put her finger to her lips in acknowledgment and continued to stroke Poe.

"No noise, Poe," Beth prayed. "Not now."

Poe poked his nose up out of the blanket. Tess murmured to him, soothing, beseeching, her panicked gaze riveted on Beth's. One small sound and they would be discovered.

The cart slowed, stopped. Bud got off.

Cold sweat dampened Beth's brow. She heard the crunch of boots as Bud approached the door.

Her blood pumped in slow motion. He stopped. The angle of the shutters prohibited him from seeing Tess lying helpless on the floor. He moved to the door.

Poe shoved more of his head out of the blanket. Would

he hear Bud? Let out one of his shrill yelps? She had no weapon to defend them. No way to summon Jack.

She hardly dared breathe as the handle rattled, Bud testing the lock.

Poe jerked a look toward the sound. Tess jiggled him in a last-ditch effort.

Quiet, baby, just for a little longer.

Her whole body was wire taut as the pup squirmed in Tess's arms. Just when she thought Poe would let loose, a radio crackled from outside and she heard Bud moving fast, lumbering back to the cart where he'd parked it. The voice over the radio was low and staticky. Male, definitely. A Cumberland, had to be, but she couldn't be sure which one of the brothers was speaking. She pressed her ear to the jamb.

"Relax," Bud said. "Gate codes are overridden and only you have control, as per your request. No one is getting out. Texts might still work in a few spots in this dump but that's a needle in a haystack situation. No phone service thanks to the electric fences and I killed the router. The problem is contained."

There was a pause, then a quiet response that ended with, "not paying you for loose ends."

"It's contained, like I said. Doesn't matter if there's a platoon of people in here hiding and for how long. Fire crews are busy trying to defend the nearby towns. Once the flames take hold, there won't be any evidence left and if there is, you can bulldoze the whole place as if you're preparing to rebuild, and no one will ever know." He paused. "The cars have been taken care of. No sign they were even here."

Beth strained to hear more.

"Nothing will turn up to incriminate you because no one's looking anymore. It's been seven days. The girl's dead by now. That's what comes of being too good at your job. She should have stopped digging."

Tess pressed a shaking hand to her mouth. Beth too was sickened at what they were hearing.

"She'll burn up with the rest of them," Bud said.

They'd been correct about the planned arson. Bud was the inside man to make sure they were all locked in place.

She caught the last two-word comment over the radio.

"No survivors."

The next few seconds Bud turned away and she couldn't hear until he reoriented.

"There won't be anyone left to talk. Your plan still holds." He laughed. "I guess smarts doesn't run in the family. Saw Ray rushing over to his trailer to pack up as if he's gonna make it to the bank to cash out. Hasn't figured out he's trapped. Dead man packing." Bud laughed some more.

Beth saw Tess's surprise that matched her own. The brothers weren't working together against Daniel?

"Gonna go check the storage room, then the office."

Office. Beth's stomach dropped.

The cart rumbled away.

She quickly crawled over next to Tess. "Did you hear what I did?"

"Uh-huh. Bud must be working for Wyatt. Ray doesn't know he's being double-crossed. But Jack…"

Beth nodded. "I have to go warn him. I don't want to leave you here alone, but…"

Tess waved her comment away. "You'll need to move quickly and I can't go that fast. Poe will stay with me."

Beth's insides twisted but she knew there was no other way. She had to get to Jack before Bud did.

"I'll be back as soon as I can, okay?"

Tess nodded and they gripped hands.

Arthur was already at the door as if he understood the urgency. She let them out and they took off at a sprint, skirting the long pathway that led to the bumper cars and a shed set back under the cover of some ragged palms.

Arthur slowed and looked aside, nose quivering as he tracked a scent that caught his attention.

"Follow," she told him firmly. There was not a second to spare if they were to reach Jack before it was too late.

Jack thanked God for Tess as he slid the key into the office lock.

He didn't risk turning on a light so he shone his penlight around the space. Three desks, a computer and printer. What he'd give to have a snoop around but at the moment, all that mattered was getting a signal.

He pulled out Beth's cell and unlocked it with Adam's birthday. Breath held, he watched it glow and checked the bars. Incredulous, he saw the no-signal indicator. No Wi-Fi to plug into either? Maddened, he looked around the space and quickly found the problem. The router had been tossed on the floor, the cords cut neatly through. He felt like hollering at the madness. Why would the brothers disable their own communications system in a locked office? Had they been afraid Daniel might arrive early for their meeting? They wanted no chance he'd be able to call for help before they killed him?

He tried to send a text, but the swirling dots indicated that wasn't going to work either. He was beginning a search for a good old-fashioned landline when he heard stealthy footsteps.

He was reaching for a heavy long-armed stapler to defend himself with until he heard Beth whisper.

"Jack."

The nerves all over his body fired into action as he hurried to unlock it. Beth wouldn't have come unless...

"Bud's coming," she said, half falling over the threshold with Arthur at her heels. "He's—"

"Back door."

"No time. I can hear him."

"Hide." He yanked out the desk chair and she and Arthur slid under the desk just as the door opened and the lights blazed on.

There was no mistaking the look on Bud's face as he glowered at Jack.

No gloating.

No satisfaction.

Just deadly fury.

Jack stepped in front of the desk to block Bud from seeing Beth.

Bud didn't waste words. He simply pulled out his Taser and fired but Jack was anticipating and he dove to the side. Scrambling to his feet, he grabbed a waste paper basket and sent it flying at Bud's face.

Bud knocked it aside and reached in his pocket for another Taser cartridge. Before he could ram it home, Jack dove for him, headfirst. Bud darted backward and finished loading his weapon. He reached up to fire it again when Beth and Arthur sprang from their hiding spot. Beth was shouting at full volume and Arthur barked in accompaniment. The movement and sound caught Bud unaware and he sidestepped and aimed the Taser at Beth.

Arthur clamped onto his wrist, slobber flying everywhere as he gripped Bud's flailing arm.

Jack dove for Bud's legs and sent him crashing backward. Bud's skull hit the floor hard and he groaned, but continued to struggle. Jack used his weight to pin his foe in place.

Beth grabbed a roll of mailing tape from the desktop and began to wrap it around Bud's ankles while Jack and Arthur kept Bud's hands still.

When his feet were restrained, she yanked the Taser from his hand and called Arthur off. The dog let go, panting and quivering.

Beth shot him a worried look while she helped Jack restrain the dazed Bud. She produced some zip ties and they pulled his hands behind his back and used another to fasten him to the metal leg of the heavy desk.

Beth hurried to Arthur, caressing and comforting him. "Oh, my sweetie. Are you okay?"

"Did he hurt himself?" Jack said, panting.

"I don't think so. I never imagined he'd actually attack."

"He'd do anything to protect you." And Jack felt a kinship with the old dog. He knew he'd do anything for Beth too.

Bud glared at them. "Touching scene. I'm all teary-eyed over here."

"Those are sore loser tears," Jack said. "On account of you're tied up like a nice roast, ready to go in the oven."

Bud's expression turned grim. "If you only knew."

"That you're intending to start a fire and burn the place down? We do know that."

Bud shook his head and yanked on the desk, which didn't give an inch. "You're going to die, you know, unless you let me go. All the gates are secured with codes. I can override them."

"Don't bother. We'll climb over."

Bud laughed, a chuckle that turned into a guffaw. "I don't think so, wiseacre. Guess what? Electric fence was activated as of an hour ago. I'd love to see you try and get over that."

"We'll find a way," Beth said, paling.

"No, you won't."

Beth shook her head at him. "So all this is because Tess discovered Wyatt and Ray were stealing from Daniel?"

"Now why would you think a thing like that?"

"Attacking the accountant Daniel hired and leaving her for dead sort of led us in that direction," Jack said. "No honor among thieves, is there? They don't want big brother to sort them out at the meeting tonight and they intend to be long gone before that happens. And your job was to make sure Tess didn't fill him in beforehand."

Bud laughed again. "So smart, aren't you? Did you want me to pat you on the head and give you a lollipop?"

"Too bad things didn't go to plan. We haven't found Daniel yet, but we will."

"Don't think so."

"Are you working for Ray? Wyatt? Or both of them."

"I heard him talking to Wyatt," Beth said. "I don't think Ray knows what his brother's up to."

Bud stayed silent.

"We have more time to search for answers now that you're going to stay out of our hair. Have fun holding up the desk." He took Bud's cell phone. "Unlock it for me."

Bud spat. Jack narrowly avoided the flying saliva.

"You're so smart you figured it all out, huh?" Bud said. "Don't need me to help with the loose ends. I'm just here for the cash."

"Well, you're not going to collect on your paycheck. Tell me where Daniel is." If there was a chance to save him, he'd do what he could after he got the women and dogs out.

Bud glared at them. "Thought you were the brains of this operation. He's dead, Einstein."

Beth's eyes flew wide. "Why? You could have just dumped him like you did with Tess and Jack."

Bud scoffed. "What difference does it make? Like I said.

I'm just here for the cash. I don't care who pays me and I don't care who dies."

Jack pulled another strip of tape loose from the roll and smiled. "That's enough talking for now. Can't have you yelling out for Wyatt, can we?"

Bud squirmed. "Come on now. Let's quit playing around. You aren't going to leave me here."

"Why not?" Beth said. "We'll send the cops when we can."

Bud flinched. "That'll be too late. He's going to burn the place down."

"Which he?"

Bud's face went red as Jack approached with the tape. "You'll all die. If you let me go I'll get the code. Disarm the fence. We can all make it out."

"We will, but not with the help of a sellout like yourself." Jack slapped the tape over Bud's mouth, which muffled his stream of obscenities.

"Take a look at this." Jack pointed to a schematic posted on the wall. "Those are the security camera locations. Entrances and exits and the gift shops. Minimal coverage probably due to cost."

"So we don't have to worry about them tracking our location unless we're in those areas?"

"Yes, ma'am. Not much help, but something until we figure out how to breach the gates."

"Do you think he's telling the truth about the gate codes and electrified fence?"

"We'll check that, soon as we can."

"Bud said 'he' not 'they,' which seems to confirm the brothers aren't working together. Sure felt like they were at first. They might both be guilty, though."

"One is backstabbing the other? What a family."

Jack reported on the lack of signal as he peeked through the window shades.

"Still cut off from help." Beth chewed her lip as she called to Arthur and they snuck out the door, locking it behind them.

Arthur moved slowly, as if he'd strained every muscle defending Beth. Jack thought for a moment. "How about we score some wheels, buddy? My feet are tired too."

Beth arched a brow.

"Why walk when we can ride?" He grinned. "No cameras operational here, right?"

Beth's smile was deeply grateful. "There's a little space heater mounted on the dash. We can warm up Arthur, Poe and Tess."

"Traveling in luxury, I like it. How's Tess?"

Beth lost her smile as he helped her lift Arthur carefully into the back seat of the cart. "She needs an IV, probably antibiotics. Feverish and weak."

The urgency was clear. The minutes were rushing by and they were no closer to escaping. He pressed the gas and they flew back to the grilled cheese shack.

When they entered, Poe yipped a hello from his spot under Tess's chin. She raised her head. "Is help on the way?"

"Not exactly." Jack reluctantly reported their failure to send a message and the encounter with Bud. It pained him to see the hope die in her eyes. "But we have some useful intel and Bud has been neutralized. So we're down to Wyatt, unless Daniel plays into this somehow."

Beth turned to Tess. "Do you think Wyatt is behind it all?"

"I do," Tess said. "One time I saw Ray looking through the papers on Wyatt's desk, like he didn't trust him. When he saw me watching he laughed it off. Said he had to keep an eye on his little brother in case he started making plans without him."

"Apparently Wyatt did just that." Jack frowned. "But everyone's an enemy until we're shown otherwise. At the core, they were both stealing from the third brother, who is likely dead, if Bud is telling the truth."

"A big 'if,'" Beth said.

"Like I said, everyone's an enemy. Our long-range plan is the same. We get to the back exit. It's the closest. If Bud's telling the truth, we won't be able to use the gate, so we'll have to find the utility shed and shut down the power and climb over."

Both women looked at him with mirrored expressions of doubt, but neither voiced their misgivings. He had them too, but there was no choice. He didn't add the rest of his musings. It required only one person to get out and alert the authorities. The other had to stay back with Tess.

His plan was for Beth to go. She was fit and fast. He'd stay and protect Tess and the dogs with his last breath.

Beth was staring at him as though she realized he was working on a secret plot, so he smiled. "Ready to roll? We can take the cart until we're in range of the cameras."

"And then?"

"Then we'll probably need a diversion."

"Such as?"

"One issue at a time, Ms. Wolfe."

Only they had way more than one to fight through.

Arthur looked up from his examination of Poe, his nose damp from the water Beth had provided. He whined, a soft sound full of concern.

I'm right there with you, buddy.

TEN

Beth helped Tess to the front seat of the security cart and aimed the heater squarely at her.

"That feels glorious," Tess said, one hand clutching Poe and the other pressed close to the heater. Poe basked in the warmth as well. The miniscule dog seemed in better shape than his companion, and Beth decided they would need to try more hydration and food at regular intervals no matter what.

Arthur seemed agitated, reluctant to get into the back seat with her. Beth worried he'd possibly injured himself or aggravated his arthritis with his surprise attack on Bud, but he didn't show any tension in his limbs or signs of outright pain. She finally coaxed him in and gave him a few jerky treats and handed some up to Poe who snarfed them eagerly.

"Eyes peeled, okay?" Jack said.

Tess nodded and scanned out her side of the vehicle while Beth did the same. The brothers were in the park, unless they'd both departed without being observed. Was that an actual possibility? That with Bud tied up there were no more human threats? Ray and Wyatt might have decided independently their plans had gotten so far off the rails the best solution was escape. And Beth wasn't sure she believed that the fence was now electrified and the codes overridden either, but she knew Jack meant to test it out.

For now, he kept to the paths where they had noted there was no camera coverage. The drifting smoke from the wildfire was thick, burning her nostrils and depositing ash on every surface. The cart carried them into the desert-themed quadrant, where the decor shifted to camels and cacti. Arthur's nose continued to quiver and his head swiveled back and forth causing his ears to swing like pendulums. She stroked his neck to try and soothe him. The poor old dog should have been snoozing and playing with other dogs at the training conference, not trying to keep his master and her companions alive.

Jack paused to survey the area before they rolled onto a service road behind a quad with a bumper car ride on one side and a bank of shrubbery on the other. It was the last outpost before they'd encounter the back lot and the rear exit. And they'd also be within view of the cameras at that point for anyone watching to see. She felt prickles run up and down her spine. He pulled the cart off the road into the shadows and parked, got out his binoculars and trained them in the trees and beyond.

While she tried to calm Arthur, she took in the tangled shrubbery that was threatening to engulf the service road. Obviously the landscape maintenance had been neglected for months. Through the haze, she noticed a pair of metal utility doors set into a concrete block in the ground just to their right, approximately five feet square.

Likely it was a place to conceal the network of wires or perhaps a pump system that served the park. She wouldn't have given it a second glance except for the stout piece of wood shoved through the two handles, jamming them closed from the outside.

Beth stared. Odd, wasn't it? Arthur whined.

"Why exactly would someone do that?" she said, pointing to the panels. "I could see locking it to prevent the public from opening it, but why do it that way? With a piece of wood?"

As Jack turned to look, Arthur broke from her grasp and bounded out of the cart.

She dashed from the vehicle and gave chase, catching hold and hauling him to a stop inches from the metal panel.

"What's gotten into you, honey?" she said.

Jack and Tess were coming to join her.

"Whatcha got, P.?" Jack said. His tone was teasing but his expression wasn't.

"There's a—"

Tess gasped, her terrified gaze riveted to the trail behind them.

"He's coming," Tess called, face chalk white.

Beth looked wildly around, seeing nothing.

"I saw him," Tess interrupted, pointing to the fringe of shrubbery. "Ray. Running along the path toward us."

Ray? Not Wyatt? Everyone's an enemy until proven otherwise, Jack had warned.

Arthur's big ears flapped in agreement. Someone was approaching for sure, and they were close, judging from the sounds. The three were too far from the cart now and they couldn't run back to where Jack had concealed it without being seen or intercepted.

She scanned in all directions. There was nothing to hide behind.

Jack pointed and they raced to the quad and sprinted into the bumper car ride. She prayed no one was monitoring the cameras. It was dark under the oval roof, the slick floor a shiny arena housing the two dozen bumper cars, painted in desert camouflage patterns.

"Scatter," Jack said.

She and Arthur hopped onto the floor, scurrying between the individual cars.

The crunch of footsteps told her Ray was almost upon them. She couldn't see Jack and Tess anymore. Arthur's nails clicked on the hard surface. She moved to a car deepest in the shadows, one covered with yellow lightning bolts.

"In," Beth whispered to Arthur, who leapt immediately. "Low."

The dog sank down into the dark interior where he wouldn't be immediately visible, but he took up the whole space. She got into the adjacent one and ducked down, heart in her throat.

Uncertain where her companions had gone, she guessed Jack and Tess were near the small podium from which the ride was controlled.

From her fetal position, she could see a tiny slice of the entrance. Their pursuer came into view, definitely Ray Cumberland. So much for her theory that the brothers had fled the park. He moved tentatively, sweat on his forehead, his sparse hair standing up in clumps. He gripped a knife, which trembled in his hand.

A knife...

She knew enough from her two former law enforcement children that knife attacks were often deadly, even for well-trained combatants. Jack and Tess could be grievously hurt if they tried to stop Ray and she had no doubt that Jack was on his way to do just that.

Ray continued his approach, sped around the metal guardrails and stepped tentatively onto the bumper car floor.

Something moved behind Ray. Jack. She quickly lost

sight of him again. Was he aware Ray had a knife? *Don't, Jack. He'll kill you.*

"I know you're in here," Ray said. "I've been trying to find you."

Ray's voice startled Arthur but he stayed quiet.

"You can't get out. The gate codes are changed and the fence is electrified." His voice was high-pitched and unsteady. He'd lost the bravado he'd displayed when he confronted them at the front gate. Worried now? Was he aware his brother was working against him?

Ray took another few steps, moving through the bumper cars, checking them one by one as he advanced. "Come out and we can talk. That's all I want. You too, right?"

She held her breath as the rubber soles of his shoes squeaked. Closer now. Where was Jack?

Ray's shadow moved over the car next to hers. Close. She squished down as far as she could go but at the last second he turned away. She realized with a flash of fear he was standing over the car where Arthur was hiding. The dog was gangly and awkward. He was easily visible and there was no way he could rally a response like he had in the office. Her precious old dog would not be able to defend her or himself.

"I'll kill him if you don't come out," Ray said slyly, only feet from her hiding spot.

Beth sat up in the car. "Do not touch my dog," she snarled.

Ray jolted and swiveled to her, eyes huge. "Where's the guy with you? The investigator?"

"I don't know."

But she saw Jack approaching, darting in between the bumper cars to get to them. She had to keep Ray talking.

"You and your brother are criminals."

Ray scraped a hand over his sweating scalp. "If you'd

just left things alone," he said. "Left when Wyatt came after you. None of this would have happened."

"Get away from her." Tess's voice rang out shrill across the space.

Ray jerked in surprise and dropped the knife, which skittered under a nearby car.

Beth saw now that Tess was clinging to the ride operator's podium with Poe tucked under her elbow. Poe howled and Arthur joined in, filling the space with noise.

Ray's gaze locked on Tess. His mouth fell open and he gaped. "I…thought you quit."

"Oh, sure you did," Tess called out. "You were completely unaware I was dumped in the tunnel underneath the roller coaster and left to die because I found out you two were stealing." Her voice was sharp with anger.

"I… I didn't do that," Ray said. "Wyatt—"

Tess's eyes burned. "None of it's your fault, is it? Just like you aren't a liar and you didn't have anything to do with killing Daniel. Spare me."

Ray made a move but Tess pushed a button and slammed her palm on the control panel. The bumper cars lurched into motion, fake headlights flashed and a tinny music blared out. The car nearest Ray spun awkwardly and knocked into him, sending him stumbling. Beth tried to keep him in sight as her car began to spin in dizzying circles.

Arthur and Poe yowled in accompaniment and Beth hung onto the side, trying to get her bearings. Electronic music nearly deafened her. The car swung around in a circle and she twisted to keep Ray in focus.

Jack leapt over the nearest car and charged toward Ray, but he had to dive around an oncoming bumper as he struggled to keep his footing. Ray was fast and agile and well-acquainted with the bumper cars from the look of it.

He scrambled off the floor, hurtled over the railing and sprinted from sight. Jack started to go after him when he was knocked over by another circling bumper car. She was flung back against the seat of her own.

Tess pushed a second button and the ride abruptly stopped. Beth shook her head to clear it just as Jack got to his feet. Arthur stared dizzily at her.

Jack helped her from the car. Her legs wobbled and he pulled her close, steadying her. She pressed her forehead to his shoulder.

"I thought he was going to stab you," she breathed.

"Ditto," Jack said, his voice hoarse. "You okay?"

"Shaken like a snow globe, but okay."

He breathed out a long, slow sigh and held her close. She pressed her forehead to his chest. If they could only stay that way, just for a minute... But she couldn't indulge in such comforts.

They hurried to Arthur, Beth assisting him from the cramped space.

Arthur stared at his paws as if to make sure the floor wasn't still moving. "It's okay, Lovebug. We've stopped spinning."

Jack retrieved Ray's dropped knife and they both hurried to Tess, who smiled in spite of her pallor.

"You two saved the day," Beth said, giving Poe a quick pat.

Tess grinned. "Surprised you, huh?"

"Absolutely," Jack said. "You moonlight as a ride operator when you're not balancing the books?"

Tess chuckled. "On my free time I strolled the park. I saw how they worked the machines and sometimes I even took a little ride or two. Good thing, right? Came in handy just now."

Beth thought of Ray's sharp blade. "Yes, good thing. Do you believe what Ray said? That he didn't dump you down there?"

Tess shook her head. "He's a thief and a liar so naturally he'd blame Wyatt."

Beth exchanged a glance with Jack. "But he looked shocked as anything to see you. And he didn't exactly have the actions of a stone-cold killer. His hands were shaking."

"I'm not an investigator, but after what I've been through, I don't think either one is capable of being truthful." Tess shivered and clung to the podium for support.

Beth put an arm around her and helped her out of the ride area.

"He said we should have left things alone and cleared out when Wyatt first threatened us," Beth said.

Jack looked around carefully before they darted across the path toward the cart. "They were in league up to that point, one assumes, until they turned against each other."

Jack urged Tess toward the passenger seat. "We have to get out of here quickly before Ray rallies."

Beth didn't need any encouragement.

"Up, Arthur," she said, patting the back seat of the cart.

The dog remained where he was, bloodshot eyes fixed on hers. Disobedience? Arthur hadn't ever exhibited such behavior in his life. She repeated the command. Arthur again did not budge. "What's gotten into you?"

She tried to lift him up but he backed out of her hold. Instead he went to Tess, pawed at her leg, stood on his hind paws until he stood face-to-face with her, snuffling her chin.

"Arthur, down," Beth said sternly. He withdrew to a sitting position and flapped his ears. She reached for him and he edged away, continuing to retreat from her until his tail brushed the metal panel with the wood plank jammed between them. He shook his whole body, sending the flaps of skin in motion.

He barked, circled and barked again.

Beth's stomach sank as she watched.

"Why is he so interested in those panels?" Tess said.

She blew out a long slow breath. "I'm afraid."

Tess frowned. "To know what's inside?"

Not what, she thought. *Who.* Bud was accounted for and they'd just scared Ray away. Had they just found the spot where Wyatt had dumped his brother Daniel?

Or were there other grisly mysteries left to be discovered?

But Arthur was tense and focused and she knew there was no choice.

They would have to find out what Arthur already knew.

Jack touched her shoulder. "All right. I'll open it. You two sit in the cart with the dogs and keep a lookout."

Beth understood that Jack was worried about what they would find too.

But worry or not, Arthur was not abandoning his post and she wasn't leaving Arthur or Jack to face whatever lay ahead alone.

"Tess can keep watch. We're staying put."

Jack rubbed his hands together to warm them.

"I hope we're not going to regret this, P," he said.

Me too.

But Arthur's gaze was steadfast and encouraging. Whatever he was trying to tell her, she had to listen.

Beth and Arthur were immovable objects, but Jack persuaded Tess to sit in the cart from which she could see them and at least yell if Ray or Wyatt appeared. Tired and sick as she was, she would be a stalwart lookout. She was Beth's equal in the determination department and that pleased him. Adam and Tess would be a marvelous couple.

Jack wondered whether his son might be worrying about the lack of contact from his girlfriend and now his father. Perhaps he'd called the police, tried to persuade them to investigate. It had to be maddening from such a long distance.

He seized the wood, which had been jammed in so tight it might as well have been a metal bar soldered in place. Heaving on it did no good so he tried kicking it from one side to force it through. He wasn't accomplishing anything until Beth took the other end, pulling as he kicked with all his might. Together, they moved it an inch. With a new flood of energy, they kept it up until the wood finally came loose.

One metal panel was stuck fast but the other opened up with a squeal. He looked in cautiously, Beth peering in over one of his shoulders and Arthur over the other. Nothing but a cold, impenetrable darkness. He crouched and aimed the flashlight Beth handed him.

"There's a short five-step ladder that leads to a type of neat little tunnel. It slopes steeply downward until it's out of view but it looks like it runs quite a distance. Probably a utility corridor of some kind." His pulse ticked up at the discovery. An underground corridor? A possible escape?

"Does it lead under the fencing? Out of the park?" Beth said, excitement building in her voice.

"Probably." He leaned farther in while she held his belt to steady him. "But there's a metal screen door-type thing about six feet in which appears to be padlocked."

"We've handled locks before."

"We sure have." He thought about the implications. If there was a secret entrance in and out of the park, they'd be able to bypass the security gate and cameras and sneak out without being seen. Which raised the second question. Were the brothers accessing it too? And who'd jammed it closed?

Arthur shoved his floppy muzzle into the space and barked once before Beth hurried to quiet him.

"Not going to know for sure until I go down there."

"We," Beth corrected.

He'd had a feeling she'd say that. "Let's fill Tess in."

They hurried to the cart.

"Fifteen minutes," he told Tess. "We'll allow ourselves that much time to try and pick the lock. If you see Ray or Wyatt, yell for us and if they're too close get yourself out of here on the cart. Find someplace to hide. If we can get away, we'll rendezvous at the back gate exit."

What a plan, he thought. Utterly desperate. Was this a smart risk to take? He wasn't convinced any of it was an acceptable risk for Tess and Beth, but there was little he could do to protect them.

With Arthur on his shoulders, he climbed down the ladder, releasing the dog to turn and help Beth, who did not need assistance as she descended lightly after him.

The cold was more intense, numbing his extremities.

Beth skimmed her fingers over the wall and found a switch, which she flipped. A single light bulb fizzed to life and they blinked.

As he'd thought, about fifteen feet beyond where they were standing was a sturdy wire gate barring the way, a thick padlock gleaming. There would be no getting through that with Beth's pry tool, but maybe they might find a handy pair of bolt cutters nearby.

He started to move toward the gate when Arthur stopped him with a sharp bark.

He looked at Beth. "What's he trying to tell us?"

She pointed.

A small door recessed into the wall marked Storage was the object of Arthur's attention.

Arthur started to bound over to it, but she held on to his collar. "Whatever he's been reacting to is in there."

An answer to a question he didn't want to ask. Jack nodded, put a finger to his lips and crept forward. Arthur's tension increased and Jack felt the hairs on his arms stand up.

With a yelp, Arthur broke free and ran to the door, circling as was his training and sitting, eyes so focused he saw nothing else.

In there, he seemed to say. *Hurry.*

But if Jack's suspicions were true, they would find Daniel in a grave condition. The man hadn't called out or made any kind of noise when he heard them enter. The brothers would have made sure their eldest sibling was taken care of permanently. But they'd found Tess alive, hadn't they? He pulled on the handle. It stuck at first, but came loose with a squeal. Arthur whined and strained to get inside, but Beth held him back.

The tiny room had upper shelves filled with cleaning products. Below was a large, rectangular rolling trash receptacle. Jack saw nothing out of place. Was it possible whatever had been in the space was no longer there?

Arthur was done being patient. He shoved his way around Jack and pawed at the receptacle. Jack took a cautious look. His heart turned to ice. The blood roared in his ears. It could not be. It must not.

"What?" Beth cried.

He was unable to answer or she couldn't hear him over Arthur's agitation.

She surged forward to see for herself.

"No, Beth." He shot out a hand to prevent her but she

was already there, looking inside, seeing the sight he would never, ever purge from his memory.

A figure lay curled up inside.

A man.

With Jack's dark thatch of hair, matted with blood.

Inside was their son.

Adam.

ELEVEN

Jack's body moved on automatic pilot while his mind blared at him like a siren. Beth appeared paralyzed, breathing hard, holding Arthur close as she stared in horror.

Her voice was husky, almost unrecognizable. "Is that…?"

Arthur yowled, a long mournful peal.

He couldn't tell her, but she knew, probably because the hair and profile exposed to their view looked so much like his.

"No!" Beth's words were a cry and she began to pray aloud while he worked on their son.

As gently as he could, he hauled Adam from the garbage bin and laid him down on the floor. Beth should be conducting the assessment, with her medical skills, but he could not have her be the one to discover the worst, so he pressed his fingers to his son's throat and prayed.

At first, he felt nothing. Soul-deep terror threatened to choke him. He fought it down and tried again. A flutter of a heartbeat, an answered prayer. "He's breathing and he's got a pulse."

Beth sank to her knees and began to examine him for herself. Her fingers trembled. "He's had a blow to the back of his head." As she continued the exam, Arthur slathered a tongue along the side of Adam's cheek. There was no re-action.

Arthur twisted toward a sound. Jack had not a moment to react before Tess clambered down the ladder, clutching Poe.

"I heard Arthur howling. I had to come. What's wrong?" Her gaze finally fastened on their fallen son. Her face went slack and she wailed, dropping to her knees. "That's not Adam. That can't be him. Please tell me it's not him."

He moved to comfort her but she crawled forward on hands and knees "Adam!" she cried out, grasping his hand. Poe yowled in uncertainty. When Adam didn't move, she appealed to Beth. "How badly is he hurt? He can't be… I mean, he's not…" She broke into shuddering sobs.

Jack gripped her wrist and firmly moved her away a few feet. "Tess, listen to me. He's alive."

"Alive?" she whispered.

Jack repeated it, still holding on to her. "Take a deep breath. I'll stay right here with you while Beth checks him. She knows what to do."

Together they watched as Beth examined Adam further for outward signs of injury while he patted Tess's hand to keep her calm. A big feat, since his own heart was threatening to crack through his ribs.

"How? How did he get here?" Tess sobbed. "I thought he contacted you to find me. He's supposed to be overseas on the oil rig. Not here in this awful place." She began to sob again.

Jack clutched her tighter. "We don't know. There's no way to ascertain that, but he's alive and we have to keep him that way. That's what matters right now."

Tess nodded slowly. "What can I do?"

"Can you distract Arthur so Beth has more room to ma-neuver?"

The question seemed to galvanize her into pulling herself together. With soft entreaties and gentle pressure, she urged Arthur to the far side of the corridor. Now that the bloodhound had found his quarry, he was compliant enough to obey. Tess laid Poe next to Arthur and he began to lick his little protégé.

Beth's voice was tight but in control when she finally spoke again. "His vitals are steady. I suspect his wrist is broken so I've stabilized it as best I can. No outward sign of bleeding except from a laceration on his forehead." She reached out to touch Adam but stopped before she made contact, staring, dazed.

Jack placed his palm on her shoulder and she gripped his hand hard. "Our son," she whispered. "This is our son."

He could only return the pressure and try to accept the terrible new reality. Their son was here. His girlfriend too. Beth and the dogs. The situation was spinning ever more into chaos. So many lives at stake and he was desperate to get them out. But how?

When she pulled a package of wipes from her pack and began to cleanse the blood from Adam's brow, he hurried to the gate and checked it thoroughly to make sure it was locked as he'd supposed. The latch and grid were made of strong metal, solidly welded. The padlock threaded through the handle wouldn't yield. He looked longingly through the passageway, positive it led to freedom outside the park. He could see the tracks made by vehicles that had traversed the tunnel while tending the underground conduits. The employees had to have entered and exited from the outside. He yanked on the lock, the clang making Tess jump. Their escape route was tantalizingly close, but maddeningly out of reach.

Even though he returned and ransacked the storage closet, there was nothing he could use to cut through the lock.

Options. There had to be a way to find a cutting tool on the property.

The utility shed in the back lot could hold the solution. From there he might be able to find a tool that would help him get through this padlock or perhaps even locate the master panel to deactivate the electric fence. Either way, the answer was to get Beth and Tess and the dogs out safely.

And he would protect Adam from the killer brothers until help arrived. Beth wasn't going to accept his decision, but he would force her to. Adam was over six feet tall and solid, too heavy for Jack to carry out without compromising everyone's escape.

This time he knew what was best for her and their son, and God would help him see it through. He would defend Adam until his last breath if it came to that. Tess startled him from his thoughts with a question.

"How did Arthur know Adam was down here? The dog's never even been around him."

Beth's gaze roved over Tess, who toyed with her necklace. "Arthur was interested in your jewelry. I'm going to guess it's from Adam?"

Tess's fingers went to the small gold cross and her expression softened. "Yes, he gave it to me as a birthday gift."

Beth's mouth trembled. "Hand delivered?"

Tess nodded. "He put it on my neck himself the day before he left for the rig."

"Arthur picked up Adam's scent and tracked it here." Beth cooed to her bloodhound and Arthur accepted the love. "If you hadn't led the way, my sweet boy..." Her comment died.

None of them wanted to think about what would have happened if Arthur hadn't followed his nose.

"We have to get Adam off this floor right away," Beth said. "It's too cold."

"It's probably safest for him to stay here for a while—you all too." He explained his plan to get to the utility room and return to cut the padlock.

Beth shook her head. "I agree with the goal, but Adam needs to be moved in the meantime, off the cement. Even a grassy area would be better than here as long as it's dry."

Jack scrubbed his hand along his five-o'clock shadow. The grilled cheese shack offered no better accommodations than their current hideout. His mind drifted to their encounter with Bud.

"The office," Tess said, as if reading his thoughts. "We still have the key."

"We've got Bud tied up there," Beth reminded him.

"There's an attached back room with a separate door. Ray would lay down on a cot there when he worked late hours. A cot would be the best thing for Adam, wouldn't it?" Tess hadn't let go of Adam's hand. Her words throbbed with hope. "He'd be warm and protected. I'll stay with him and Poe while you two go to the utility room."

"No, Tess. I—"

Tess stopped Beth's reply with a hard look. "Adam obviously left his job and came out of worry. He was attacked and dumped, all because he wanted to protect me." Tears glittered in her eyes and she blinked hard. "I'm going to stay with him every second until we get out of here or…"

Beth went to her and wrapped her in a tight hug.

The woman seemed so small, standing against the wide gray wall. Both were cold, hungry, hurting, terrified, and yet they would not bow in defeat. In two strides he drew close and wrapped them in a wide hug, his encircling arms promising what he couldn't say.

We will survive. All of us.

The dogs reacted to the group hug. In a flash, Arthur and Poe had wormed their way into the circle, all big and tiny paws and wet noses. The warmth spread through them and when he let go, he felt encouraged and more determined than ever.

"I'll climb up the ladder first with Arthur and take a look. If it's clear, then Tess and Poe can get out next. Drive the cart close as you can, Tess. Beth, I'm going to need you to help. Okay?"

Beth agreed and they put the plan in motion. Jack hoisted Arthur up the ladder. Beth called out for the dog to stay and he did so as Jack climbed down again.

Jack and Beth helped Tess, after she bundled Poe in her jacket. She was moving with more strength—a new resolution to help Adam had revived her somewhat. He was glad to see it. When she'd reached the top and gone to get the cart, Jack turned to Beth.

"All right. Help me get Adam on my shoulders."

Beth reached for their unconscious son, then stopped, her hands arrested. He didn't understand until he realized how huge a moment it must be for Beth. The last occasion she'd lifted Adam had been to give him away to another family to raise.

He turned her until they were face-to-face and cupped her cheeks. "God's given you back your son."

She battled the tears. He did too. This was a moment he never could have imagined in his wildest dreams. He and Beth, working together, for the good of their child. The emotion he felt was overwhelming.

He leaned in and kissed her.

Her lips were warm and yielding as she kissed him back. It felt as if a missing piece of his heart settled into place.

What did it mean? Why did he feel like he'd been raised above the floodwaters? He realized with a jolt that he was falling in love with her all over again. Pure and simple. Banged-up, torn and tattered as he was, not the young man all full of brash bravado, but humbled, imperfect, faithful and completely certain of how precious she was in his life.

How could it be happening?

She tucked her head and rested it on his chest and he gathered her close as the sharp kernel of reality settled in.

She has another life now, filled with people who love her. She won't need you after this is all over.

The thought cut to the bone, but no matter how she felt, he'd always need Beth, even if he could never have her. After one more moment, he took a deep breath, pushed away the pain and got moving.

It took both of them to work their son into a manageable position. Adam was heavy, but Jack locked his knees and levered the weight forward. He took the ladder slowly, Beth climbing behind him, supporting Adam's back. Tess hovered at the entrance and the three of them managed to pull Adam free before they climbed out and worked together to load their patient across both back seats. Their four-passenger ride could no longer accommodate them all.

"You drive, Beth," Jack said. "I'll walk alongside with Arthur."

She complied. Tess twisted in the passenger seat so she could keep eyes on Adam as they rolled along.

The smoke lay in pockets across the path. It was late afternoon, but oddly dark, the winter sun completely cloaked in smoke as it began to descend toward the horizon. His nose and eyes burned from the foul air. In order to avoid the zone that might be covered by the cameras, they chose the outer path that led them closer to the perimeter of the park. He prayed they'd be able to stay undetected as they worked their way toward the office again.

It was quiet enough now to hear the soft hum of the fence off to their right. His spirit sank a notch. If he'd had any doubts about the truth of Bud's statement, he didn't any longer. The fence really had been activated, only now it was certainly not to keep people out, but in.

The Cumberlands were a murderous family, consumed by greed and desperation and it had made them utterly without limits as they tried to cover their tracks, together or separately. The cart trundled into a copse of spindly eucalyptus. The towering trees thrust their branches up into the poisonous sky. Meant to create shade and soften the view of the fence, now they added to the menacing gloom.

Arthur woofed softly. Beth slowed, came to a stop.

"Jack…" Her attention was riveted to something ahead.

Jack tensed as he too noticed the bundle lying at the foot of one slender tree trunk.

"What is that?" Tess half whispered.

The drifting smoke caught on the shape that he didn't at first recognize. Perhaps a trick caused by the foul air? A fallen branch twisted in the shape of a…

Body?

He swallowed and crept forward cautiously as Beth put Arthur into a stay.

The closer he drew, the more the bile rose in his throat.

A man lay in the road, unmoving, lifeless.

Ray Cumberland.

Jack took in Ray's head twisted almost backward on his crumpled body, his sightless eyes staring up into the haze.

Beth steeled herself not to shake as her examination of Ray confirmed her suspicion. "He's dead," she said. "His neck is broken and the back of his skull is caved in."

Jack helped her to her feet and they returned to the cart.

Tess hugged herself. "This is a nightmare. What happened to him?"

Jack eyed the tree. "Looks like he tried to climb the tree and jump over the fence but he fell."

"Why would he think that would work?" Tess said.

Beth shook her head. Only desperation would lead a person to attempt such a plan. Now with the discovery of her wounded son, her own tide of desperation was rising rapidly. "But it confirms what we suspected. Ray wasn't working with Wyatt on this scheme. He didn't know the codes to enable his escape so he tried to get out on his own." A waste of a life, she thought.

There was nothing to be done but to say a prayer for the dead man and restart their journey, a deadly silence falling over the little group. With Ray deceased, they had to be on the alert for Wyatt whom she worried was ready to assassinate them at any moment. Why didn't he just leave town? Get away with whatever money he could get his hands on? Was that out of the question now that Ray could not sign for the withdrawal? Maybe they'd been wrong and somehow Wyatt and the missing Daniel were in league together against Ray.

Wyatt must have another plan; he was full of them. If he succeeded in making the four of them disappear below the bowels of the park, who would ever think to look for them there? Would her children investigate? Follow the trail from the hotel to the amusement park? Would they feel betrayed that she'd gone off on her own when they thought she was safely at a bloodhound convention? Perhaps they were already looking for her—she hadn't been able to check in with them since Garrett's text at the hotel. It was a comforting thought, but she couldn't count on a rescue from her family.

As she caught a glimpse of Jack, Tess and Adam, she knew they were her family too, and in the gravest of dangers.

Keep going. It was all she could think to do.

She fought the urge to stop the cart every few seconds to check on Adam. Tess would alert them if he stopped breathing.

Then what?

CPR. Rescue breathing.

And if that didn't work?

She forced the thoughts away as they made it to the office.

A peek through the window told them Bud was right where they'd left him, secured to the desk, so they circled around the back, following Tess's directions. She parked the cart behind a pile of pallets before they let themselves into a tiny back room.

It was more storage space than anything else, but there was an old cot set up and a neatly folded blanket and pillow. The three of them carried Adam to the cot. His heels hung slightly over but they were able to get him on his back with the blanket tucked around him. Tess moved a folding chair over and deposited Poe under the blanket with Adam.

Beth tapped her phone open. Still no connection to make a call. She typed out a text for Garrett anyway.

Trapped in Meadowlands Amusement Park. Under attack from Cumberland brother. Send police and ambulance. There were a million more things to say, but she pressed Send, without much hope for success. The dots swirled for a moment.

Ping.

She gaped.

"It sent," she said, incredulous. "The text actually sent."

"Your kids know?" Jack grinned. "Then help will be rolling any second now."

But they couldn't wait on rescue, not with Adam involved.

"He's waking up," Tess said, breathless.

She hurried close, standing behind Tess as they watched Adam's eyelids flutter open.

Tess stroked his cheeks, sobbing. "Adam."

"Tess?" His face lit up with wonder.

"You're okay. You're alive," she whispered through her tears.

He smiled, reached for her and she kissed him on the lips. He clutched her hand with his uninjured one, his voice a hoarse croak. "You okay, Tess? I was worried sick."

"Yes." She sniffed. "You're going to be too. We got you out of the utility tunnel. You were locked in and unconscious."

"What?" He blinked and tried to rise but Jack restrained him. "Hold up, son. We're all safe for the moment."

His gaze darted to Jack and then to Beth and back again. "Jack?" His lips were cracked and Beth yearned to bandage the cut on his forehead but she held herself still. Though this man had come from her body, from her flesh and blood, lived in her womb and then her heart, to him she was a stranger. She stayed put, soaking in every syllable he spoke.

"I need you to fill in the gaps for me."

"I'll do what I can," Jack said. "Do you know where you are?"

Adam paused to recollect. "Meadowlands. I left my job and flew home on a red-eye. Had to." He held on to Tess. "I couldn't leave it to someone else. And then I couldn't get any messages from Jack, which confirmed my thinking. I made it here early this morning. That is, if it's still Friday."

Jack nodded. "Friday, late afternoon."

"I was approaching the front gate, I remember, calling out because it was locked and then...nothing."

"You were attacked," Tess said. "Locked up."

"By whom?" Adam asked. Beth watched the small tilt of his head as he assumed the same mannerism of his father Jack. She swallowed.

Jack quickly explained what they'd endured and the current circumstances.

Adam sighed. "So we're locked in the park?"

"Yes. We wouldn't have even known you were here if..." Jack broke off and looked at Beth.

Her heart pounded and she shook her head. *Not the time. Not at all.*

"There's someone else with us."

No, Jack, she silently pleaded.

Jack swooped an arm around her shoulders and drew her close. Adam's gaze wandered to her face, a frown on his brow.

Jack squeezed her. "This is Beth Wolfe and her bloodhound Arthur. Arthur tracked your scent using the necklace you gave Tess."

Tess brushed away some tears. "Good thing I never take it off." Her voice broke on the last word. Adam pressed her fingers and kissed the knuckles before his gaze drifted back to Beth.

"Hi," she said, but it came out in a whisper.

Adam pursed his lips and stared at her. He looked as if he were fitting together the pieces of a puzzle. "We have the same eyes."

Beth's limbs went rubbery. "I... I, um..."

"You're my birth mother, aren't you?"

She couldn't answer. Jack held her close, her body quaking. "She's been in this thing the whole time. Trying to find Tess and now you. We would have passed right by if it wasn't for her and her dog."

Still she couldn't speak, staring at the full-grown man who lay in front of her, seeing herself in some of his features, Jack in others. What would he think? What would his next comment be to her, his birth mother? The rejection would sting like nothing else. Nothing she'd done the past twenty-four hours could make up for thirty-eight years of silence. She'd chosen not to find him. What excuse could there be for that? Was she going to faint? She wasn't sure. Her blood felt like it had drained away.

Tess took a tiny step back and pressed her palms to her heart.

And then Adam reached out his free hand. To her?

She stared at it.

Jack gently nudged her forward. Trembling, she touched him and he laced the fingers of his undamaged hand with hers.

"I'm pleased to meet you, Beth Wolfe," he said softly.

"I'm… I'm so pleased to meet you too, Adam. I never thought…" And then she could not talk at all, the rush of decades of pain bottling up the words in her throat so none could escape.

His smile was so gentle, so kind. "When we get out of here, we're going to have a lot of catching up to do." He swallowed. "If you want to, I mean."

"I do want that." More than anything else in the entire world, she wanted the gift God was presenting, a chance to know her son so her heart could finally beat properly again. The tears traced hot trails down her cheeks.

She looked at her beautiful boy, grown up, the woman he loved beaming at him. She felt the pressure of Jack's touch on her back and she knew this was a moment that would be impressed onto her heart until her dying breath.

"Beth, is it okay to call you that?"

She nodded.

Adam smiled. "I know you and Jack need to go on a mission, but come back okay? We only just found each other. I don't want to lose you again."

Tears choked off her words, but she nodded, then she and Arthur followed Jack outside.

Wordlessly, Jack gathered her close and they clung together.

Her head spun. Her body was cold, then hot and shivering.

"Jack," she whispered. "Our son."

"Yes," he said, "our son."

TWELVE

Jack held Beth, absorbing as much comfort as he provided her, until she took a deep shuddering breath and pulled away.

She wiped her eyes. "We gotta get moving."

"All right." They decide to leave the cart where it was in case Tess needed to move quickly if Wyatt found them. It would likely be impossible for her to load Adam, in her weakened condition, but it made him feel better that they had the option.

He prayed Wyatt had taken what he needed and split town. All they required to go on their way was one simple thing, a bolt cutter.

He moved as fast as he dared, and Beth kept up but he could tell she was lagging too. It felt like they'd been scrambling to survive for months, instead of only a few days. As they skirted the edge of the arcade booths, he stopped. "Look."

Between the shooting gallery and the milk bottle toss was a gap that allowed them a view to the field on the other side of the electric fence. A fire burned, the flames dancing orange in the dry grass. Plumes of smoke were rising, joining with the general haze.

"And there," Beth added.

Sparks had drifted through and danced along the wood

paneling of the arcade. It wouldn't be long before the whole structure caught.

"An old amusement park, closed to the public," Jack said softly. "The fire department won't waste resources trying to save it. Far as they know, there's no one here."

"The smoke will be lethal long before the flames get us."

He had no comment for that except to start running. She and Arthur followed suit.

The sizzle and pop of sparks grew louder as they sprinted. There was no choice but to risk being captured by the cameras now as they rushed to the utility shed. The brothers' trailers were just behind, the windows dark.

He thought about Ray lying dead on the path, his desperation to escape fueling his recklessness. If he didn't get them out of the park soon, the fire would do Wyatt's job for him.

The shed was not yet wreathed in smoke as they hurried to it. He prayed it would stay that way.

"Hold on," Beth whispered, pulling him to a stop and commanding Arthur to halt. "The door's ajar."

The sound of tumbling boxes from inside indicated someone was there. Finger to his lips, he moved close enough that he could see Wyatt's stocky profile. This was it, their opportunity to take control of the situation by neutralizing their enemy once and for all.

He caught Beth's eye.

She shook her head, but he ignored her message. Instead he charged inside.

Wyatt whirled around with a gasp, a socket wrench clutched in his hand. He swung it at Jack.

Jack dodged and let Wyatt's momentum carry him off-balance. When he stumbled, Jack brought him to the ground with a quick tackle and twisted his arms behind him.

Beth and Arthur ran in.

"Get off me," Wyatt snapped through clenched teeth.

"Why?" Jack snarled, pinning him. "So you can take another lead pipe to the side of my head?"

"I'll find something to secure him," Beth said. "Arthur, stay with me."

"You should have left," Wyatt said. "Why didn't you go instead of sticking your noses into our business?"

"I don't care about your business," Jack snapped. "I came to find Tess Altman, the lady you left for dead under the roller coaster."

Wyatt froze, staring. "You don't know what you're talking about. I didn't do anything to Tess. I thought she quit. It was Ray. He did it."

Jack exchanged a look with Beth. "Easy to blame a dead guy, isn't it?"

Wyatt stopped struggling and craned his neck around. "Dead? What are you talking about?"

"Ray's dead." Beth found a coil of rope to hand to Jack. "He died trying to climb a tree to get over the fence."

Wyatt's mouth went slack. "You're making it up."

A nerve started to twinge deep down in Jack's gut. Beth handed him a length of rope that he used to tie Wyatt's hands in front of him. When he was secured, Jack allowed him to sit up.

Wyatt's expression had morphed from belligerent to hunted. Jack felt the hair on the back of his own neck lift. Why would Wyatt appear so fearful? Blame everything on his brother?

Two dangerous brothers, Jack thought, until another fact prodded him. No, there were three Cumberland brothers. He reviewed what Bud told them. He'd said Daniel was dead, but he'd also made it clear his loyalty went to the brother who would pay the most. Maybe he was paid to lie by Daniel

Cumberland himself. He locked eyes with Wyatt. "It wasn't either of you, was it?"

Beth frowned as she too put the pieces together. Her eyes went wide. "You and Ray were supposed to meet Daniel tonight."

"We weren't going to show up. We were packing our stuff to get out beforehand. Would have done it sooner but I was away setting up some new digs for myself." Wyatt started to shake and he ducked his head. "I can't believe I didn't see it."

"See what?" Jack said.

Wyatt was haggard and he spoke in a monotone. "Daniel knew. He knew all along. He set this meeting but he must have known we'd be too scared to have everything brought out into the open so he trapped us here. You all got dragged in."

Beth patted Arthur nervously. "Daniel set it all up because you were stealing from him?"

Wyatt moaned. "Daniel always said he was smarter than we were. Mr. Ivy League Education. Me and Ray were going to clean out the cash account and get out well before Daniel arrived for the meeting, but we got locked in the park after we came in to deal with you." He shot a look at Jack. "He overrode the gate code. Electrified the fence. Even disabled the Wi-Fi in the office so we couldn't use that phone or the computer to get word out. It was him. It was Daniel."

Jack looked at Beth. "We were in the wrong place at the wrong time."

Wyatt nodded distractedly. "When Bud told us there were investigators sneaking around, we figured you were digging up dirt on us. I tried to scare you off, but it didn't work. When Bud reported that you were in the park, we decided we'd take care of you until we could get away. Not to murder you, just prevent you from telling anyone until we made it out. We were going to call the cops anonymously and tell them you were in here."

"I don't believe that for a second," Jack said.

"Think what you want," Wyatt said. "What do I care?"

Beth folded her arms. "Something doesn't make sense in all this. I don't understand why Daniel would go after Tess."

Wyatt looked befuddled. "I don't either. She was digging up the dirt on us. He hired her and after the meeting she was supposed to leave anyway. No point in killing her, is there?"

"And Adam?" Beth said. "Was he just in the wrong place at the wrong time?"

"Who's Adam?"

"Not important." Jack noted the orange glow through the open shed door. "Fire's taking hold. We don't have much time."

Wyatt nodded. "I was looking for a fire extinguisher in here, or a radio."

"We're after bolt cutters." Beth continued to peer into the dark corners. "We might be able to escape via the utility passage under the park."

Wyatt brightened. "I forgot about that. It's kept locked but…" He looked helplessly around. "There are tools in here, somewhere."

"I sure don't see them," Beth said. They continued to prowl the space, combing through dusty cardboard boxes. Each minute ratcheted up Jack's urgency.

His gaze landed on a spot beyond Beth's shoulder and suddenly he knew he had to try another way.

Beth turned as he snatched the object of his attention from the wall. He examined the bundle of waxy red cylinders. "Flares."

Wyatt nodded. "For emergencies."

"I'd say this qualifies. We're going to need to divide and conquer, P."

She grew still. "What are you planning?"

"Wyatt and I are going to take a walk to the Ferris wheel."

"Why?"

"Because we're going to set off a flare so the fire department can see it and the only way to get it above the smoke is from the top of that wheel."

Wyatt groaned. "I like the escape idea better."

"Me too." Beth was gearing up for an argument. "We need to stay together, like you said."

"We will be together, but Wyatt and I have a side job first."

"No way," Wyatt said.

"Too bad you don't get a vote." Before Beth could rally a response, he hauled Wyatt to his feet, flares tucked under his arm. "You and Arthur look for the bolt cutters. Take Tess and Poe and get out. Find help. After we deploy the flares, I'll retrieve the cart and transport Adam to the tunnel if the rescue people haven't arrived. It will take us some time, but Wyatt and I can carry him out."

She shook her head. "I don't like it. We should stick together."

"We can't do that, P, and you know it." Jack took her hand and caressed it before he put it to his lips. It might have been his imagination, but he thought she bent her head to his and maybe he even felt the weight of her cheek pressing close.

"Too dangerous," she said, drawing back, her eyes shining with unshed tears. "I'm scared, Jack." It was no more than a whisper.

For her to admit that...

"But I know it's what we have to do," she finished.

He'd never in his life felt so proud of another human

being. "We're going to get through this and Adam will live to know what an incredible woman gave birth to him."

When uncertainty flicked across her face, he leaned in and kissed her, gently, tenderly. "This is going to work," he said again. "All of it. Okay?"

She looked at him, paused, and edged close and kissed him back. "Don't get yourself killed, St. James. I won't forgive you. Ever."

He saluted. "Yes, ma'am."

Tension flooding her body, Beth pawed through box after box, shelf upon shelf as she frantically searched for the bolt cutters. Her fear was like a live creature gnawing at her. Fifteen minutes passed into a half hour.

She heard the soft tinkle of music and her stomach lurched. The Ferris wheel… Jack and Wyatt must have made it there and started the massive machinery. Through the open door and the fouled air, tiny pinpricks of light shone as the wheel began to spin. Now there would be no more chance to hide.

Daniel would know as soon as the flares went up exactly where to find Jack. Maybe he already knew if he had control of the cameras. She returned to her search, the minutes flying by. She was pulling boxes over now, heedless of any noise. An old crate covered with dust fell over with a clatter, spilling the contents.

Bolt cutters! She almost kissed them.

Arthur wagged his tail at her joyful shout.

"We've got a way out now, Lovebug."

She raced out of the shed with Arthur galloping at her side. The dense smoke stung her eyes and she coughed.

"Low," she said and they both bent to keep down in the

fresher air. She covered her face with her elbow and they ran back to the office.

Arthur cocked his wrinkly head as they approached. A moment later she understood why.

She saw a dark-haired man approaching the shed, a gun in one hand. He peered through the window into the interior of the storage room where Tess and Adam were hiding.

Her heart pounded. What could she do? There was no way she'd leave them to their fate. She gripped the bolt cutters and snuck forward but a twig snapped under her foot and he swiveled to cover her with the weapon.

"Welcome," he said. "Thanks for dropping by," he called inside as he fired a shot in the air. "I'm coming in, so nobody do anything stupid. It's closing time at Meadowlands."

The blurry stripes from the flare ribboned across the park but Jack paid no attention. The moment he'd gotten Wyatt back down from the top where he'd launched the flares, he'd heard a shot from the direction of the office and now he was running full tilt. Wyatt pounded along behind him, awkward with his hands bound. He could have broken off and run somewhere to hide, but Jack didn't care.

His entire consciousness was fixed on the sound of that shot. Beth. Tess. Adam. Daniel had gotten to them. He prayed he would not be too late.

The office door was open and he edged close. Through the window he could see Daniel holding a gun on Beth, Adam and Tess.

Wyatt saw too. "We have to do something," he said. "His phone controls the fence and gate codes. He's the only way out."

Jack noticed the bolt cutters Beth must have found and dropped when Daniel caught her. Better than nothing. He hefted them. "You need to call to him. Get him to move away from them. When he comes out, I'll clobber him."

"No way," Wyatt said. "He'll shoot me dead the moment he sees me."

"Like you said, we're dead anyway if we don't get the upper hand here."

Wyatt shook his head.

"Would you rather deck him?" Jack snarled.

Wyatt sighed. "Fine." He stood to the side of the door. "Daniel, it's Wyatt. The police are on their way. It's all over for you."

Jack could see Daniel cock his head as if he was listening. "Come on in and join the fun, Wyatt."

Wyatt shook his head. "He won't come out. I have to get out of here, find a way to make it over the fence." He turned on his heel and started to run when Bud stepped around the corner, an evil grin on his face.

Jack bit back a groan.

"Well, hey, Wyatt. Jack. Long time no see." Bud's Taser was fully loaded with a fresh cartridge.

"Daniel's waiting to talk to you both." He gestured. "Drop the cutters, Jack, and get inside both of you. Conscious or not is your decision."

Jaw tight, Jack followed Wyatt into the office.

THIRTEEN

Beth bit back a groan of despair as Jack and Wyatt entered with Bud following. Daniel must have released Bud while she was returning with the bolt cutters. He'd lain in wait and she'd walked right into the web. Jack had been caught because he'd tried to help. The whole disastrous affair had been a punishment to Jack for showing up for his son. She looked at him through eyes blurred with tears, this man to whom she owed so much.

Jack returned her gaze with a look of deep pain. They were out of chances and he knew it.

Daniel's smile was wolfish. "Old home week. I'm only missing one miserable relative now. Where is little brother Ray?"

"Ray's dead," Wyatt said, face contorted with hatred. "He fell out of a tree trying to escape after you locked us in here."

"Is that right? Good. Saves me a bullet." He took in their shocked reactions. "Oh, I'm sorry. I should feel some sort of love and compassion for my kinfolk?"

"That's generally how things go with siblings," Jack said, through gritted teeth.

Beth sent a message to Jack not to aggravate the murderous man, but Jack's expression blazed with defiance.

"Sure, sure," Daniel said. "My parents would have said

the same thing. Take care of your younger brothers, Dan. Things come easy to you, but not to them, the poor unfortunates. Help them out, Dan. Do the right thing by them, Dan. Uh-huh. Quality characters, my brothers. I should take good care of them while they're busy stealing from me? Those two boneheads figured I'd never find out, but guess what? I'm a tech guy. It took me a while to get around to it, but I eventually tapped into the accounting system and noted some…inaccuracies, shall we say. It was easy from there to listen in via some well-placed cameras and mics."

"You shouldn't have been a partner anyway," Wyatt said. "Mom and Dad loved this park and you never fit in here. Always too good, too smart. We never liked you, Ray and me. You don't deserve a penny from this place."

Daniel swung a fist and caught Wyatt in the chin. His head snapped back and he crumpled to the floor.

Poe howled and Tess tried to quiet him.

"When I suspected they were stealing from my share, I hired a wonderful accountant and she confirmed it," Daniel said, giving Tess a wink. "You really are sharp, honey."

She glared. "I wouldn't have confirmed anything if I'd have known you were this kind of lowlife."

"Ouch. Unkind words." There was a hint of more violence in the comment and Beth tensed. Daniel was a hair trigger away from killing them. She had to figure out some way to prevent it.

"Why did you need to attack her then?" Adam croaked, fiery spots showing on his cheeks. He was sitting up, dark smudges under his eyes and new blood oozing from his head wound.

Tess took his hand.

Daniel smiled at Tess. "Because you're a little too good

at your job. You downloaded some documents along with the financials that would make me look bad, let's say."

Tess frowned. "I didn't notice anything."

"Not yet, but I saw your comments in the file, the questions you had noted to ask, and you would have stumbled upon it if I didn't take care of things. You downloaded copies to your computer and eventually you'd see."

"See what?" she said.

"That I falsified some paperwork to make me sole owner of the park."

Jack rolled his eyes. "Crime must run in the family. Your brothers were stealing from you so you were going to punish them. Tell me how this was all supposed to play out? Indulge my curiosity. You arranged for a meeting and what was supposed to happen when they showed up?"

Daniel laughed. "What a character study. I was positive my two cowardly brothers would bolt, rather than face the music, so I made sure to be here a few days early. I hacked into the cameras in the park so it was easy to monitor. The Cumberland boys didn't disappoint. When they started packing their trailers like rats deserting a ship, I put my plan into motion. Bud had already taken care of Tess. I intended to change the gate codes and lock them in the park but I didn't count on a private eye coming to town. Imagine my surprise when Bud filled me in on your inquiries. Wyatt spilled that you were staying at a hotel and what do you know? You showed up and snuck right in." He stared at Jack. "I told Bud to allow you entrance and then take care of things, like we had with Tess. One more body wouldn't hurt. Then he alerted Wyatt and Ray, who came running to chase you off, terrified you were after them." His eyes swiveled to Beth. "None of us knew you'd snuck in too before I locked the gates tight. It became a jolly party, didn't it?"

"Lots of witnesses," Jack said.

"Lots of bodies, you mean, but that won't be a problem. The wildfires are the perfect cover. I decided when the burn got close enough, I'd help it along with Bud's assistance. It would look like my brothers died in the fires."

"Wouldn't it have been easier just to cause a car wreck or poison their food?" Jack asked.

"No. This way I can't be blamed and no one will be around to contest that I am the sole owner of the park. I'm going to have this money pit torn down and sell the land to whatever developer is fool enough to buy it."

"That explains the stacks of newspapers under the coaster," Tess said.

Adam winced as he struggled to sit up straighter. "You saw me coming to look for Tess and took me out, didn't you?"

Daniel shrugged. "I was on my way here anyway. Saw your approach on my cell phone camera so I got here ahead of you. You were hollering through the fencing for Tess and I knew you wouldn't be easily turned away. After I 'took you out' as you put it, I carried you in through the electrical conduits that run under the fence. Plenty big enough. My brothers should have remembered that."

"This isn't going to work," Jack said. "Your plan has spun out of control. Now you're going to have six bodies to explain to the cops, presuming you let your accomplice Bud here go. Mass murder is a hard thing to sweep under the rug."

"I won't be around to have to explain it. The fires are incinerating this region and it's only natural this place will be gobbled up too. No one is going to come prowling through a burned-up park looking for victims they didn't even know were here. All I have to do is keep anyone from digging under the roller coaster long enough for the sale to go through. Then I'm off to Europe."

Bud nodded. "You gotta admit it's a great plan."

Daniel continued. "When the fire's good and crackling, I'll disable the fence and unlock the codes and Bud and I will leave. I'll come back later to identify my brothers' bodies. No one will be looking for them anyway. Neither is married. They have no family."

Except the brother who was determined to kill them.

The room was so small, crammed with seven adults and the dogs. Daniel would not miss if he fired. Adam's and Jack's eyes scanned the room, as if trying to figure a way out that wouldn't result in casualties.

Daniel went to the door and opened it and turned to Bud.

"You stay here and make sure Wyatt stays put. He's going to need to be found dead on the premises along with dear Ray if my plan is going to work out. I'll take these people underneath the coaster and kill them, one by one, dogs and all."

"That sounds like a fine plan to me," Bud said. "One nice, tidy pile."

Jack stood straighter, widening his stance slightly. Beth read his subtle movements. He was going to act.

And she was going to help him. She just had to figure out how.

"Get up," Daniel said to Adam.

"He needs help. He's injured, thanks to you." Beth went to the cot and blocked Daniel's view with her body. She grabbed the corner of Adam's blanket while she helped him up. As she did so, she shot a look at Jack.

His reaction was only a blink, but she knew he'd be ready.

Tess noticed her grip on the blanket.

In a quick movement, Beth turned on her heel, whirled the blanket around and tossed it over Daniel's head. The big man reeled backward, crashing into a stack of books that went flying.

Arthur barked in alarm as Bud lunged forward. Adam snatched up a big leather-bound volume with his good hand and flung it at Bud's head. It struck him above the brow. The man collapsed with a groan. Adam staggered back onto the cot, breathing hard.

As Daniel batted the blanket away and Jack tackled him around the knees, Tess followed up by hurling another book at Daniel. He deflected it and aimed his gun at her, still struggling to stay on his feet. Tess screamed.

Poe dove for Daniel's ankle, skidding into him and snapping his teeth into Daniel's pant leg. Jack adjusted his grip and dove on top of the murderous brother. They all went over backward.

Beth ran forward and dropped her full weight on Daniel's wrist as Jack and Daniel writhed on the ground, Poe's jaws still clenched on his clothing.

Daniel nearly tore his gun hand free, but Beth dug her fingernails into his wrist until he let go. She kicked the gun away.

Jack threw an upward punch that rocked Daniel and he stopped struggling.

The room went silent save for the sound of their panting. Poe let go and tumbled his way back to Tess. Adam stared wide-eyed at his parents. His face was deathly pale but he smiled. "Who knew I came from such sturdy stock?"

Jack and Beth shared a look.

"We did," they both said at once.

Jack went to fetch the security cart while Beth, Adam and Tess kept watch over the prisoners. Neither Daniel nor Bud could escape, since they were tied up with computer cords and their mouths secured with duct tape. Wyatt was still unconscious, and Bud dazed, but Daniel stared at them with malice. He'd refused to use his phone to override the gate codes, but Jack had forced his finger onto the button to unlock it and found the app. In a few moments, their prison doors were now unsecured. Jack had also taken Daniel's keys for good measure.

Beth looked at her son and his girlfriend, filled with admiration and awe. "You two really stepped up." Tess carried Poe to Arthur and sat with them while Beth checked on Adam. The proximity of her son turned her insides to a ball of nerves. "How are you feeling?"

He rubbed his brow. "My body is a mess, but my spirit is absolutely delighted."

She looked wonderingly at the incredible person in front of her. "I'm glad." She started to move away but he touched her forearm, stopping her cold. The feel of his fingers rocked through her.

"Got a minute?" he said.

For him? She had the rest of her life. Her nerves pounded. "Sure," she said faintly.

He stared at her as if he was trying to memorize her face. "No sense wasting time with small talk, is there?"

Uh-oh. Goose bumps prickled her skin as she nodded. "Right."

His expression was grave as he spoke. "I understand why you gave me up and I don't have any bad feelings over that. You made an unselfish choice so I could thrive."

She allowed the healing words to circle through her. "It seemed like the only way to give you what you deserved."

"I just have one question."

She swallowed, suddenly dizzy. "Ask."

"In thirty-eight years you never looked for me, did you?"

A statement and an accusation. The answer fought its way out of her mouth. "No."

"Why not?"

She was paralyzed and not a single word would come out. *Why not?*

"You were ashamed?" he suggested softly.

"Of you? No. You were perfect." So perfect. So fresh from God.

"Of yourself?"

"I was sad that I'd brought a baby into the world that I couldn't care for, but that's not why I didn't try to find you."

"Why then?"

As she searched deep down inside, she discovered the truth that she'd kept hidden even from herself. This was the moment she could finally look in the mirror without pretense or self-deception. "I thought when I gave you up I shouldn't be in your life anymore...that I'd lost the right to know you."

"Your penance."

A penance, a self-inflicted wound. Her eyes swam with tears. "Yes."

"You didn't even tell your parents you were pregnant?"

She shook her head.

"And all these years you didn't share with your family either? Jack would only tell me the bare-bones facts about you. He said you'd kept things private."

"I only told my late husband. I'm sorry. It hurt too much to talk about it. I realize now it wasn't fair to you, or them."

"Or yourself."

She blinked hard.

He reached out a hand but stopped short of contact. "You wanted better for me. I understand. And that's what I got. Amazing parents, a good life. But I always had this blank space, a space that only you could fill."

Sorrow cut like a blade. "And I should have filled it, should have reached out. I just...couldn't."

He laughed. "My mom has told me ever since I can remember that God works things out in His good timing. You remind me of her. Strong and spunky. Maybe you'll be great friends someday."

How could he offer such grace? He wasn't obligated to give it just because he came from her womb. And that was the very nature of God's grace, freely given, unearned, beautiful. "I'm so deeply grateful that I had this chance to meet you, even under these circumstances." She turned but he stopped her again.

"You say that like it's a one-off."

She stared. "I... I'm not sure what you mean."

He grasped her hand, his own nicked and scratched from his recent trauma. "How about when we get clear of this, we find a way forward, not backward?"

"Forward?" Why was her voice such a tentative squeak?

"Get to know each other, our families," he said. "I'm going to marry Tess, if she'll have me."

Tess beamed with pleasure as she stroked the dogs.

"I'd like you to be part of that, you and Jack," Adam said.

You and Jack.

Is sounded so natural, so...right.

Heart filled to bursting, she leaned down and kissed his cheek, as she had thirty-eight years before. "I would like that very much."

Adam smiled. "Me too."

She was still trying to get her breathing in order when Jack returned with the cart.

"Help is coming, I can hear distant sirens, but it may take them a while to get through the smoke. It's not safe to stay here with the fire growing." He outlined a hasty plan to ferry everyone out.

She nodded. He gave her a long look.

"You okay, P.?"

She looked straight at him. "Yes, Jack. I'm okay." At long last, God had made her whole again.

He kissed her forehead before they loaded the three prisoners on the cart, taping them securely to the side supports and pocketing extra computer cords and the remaining roll of duct tape. "Be right back."

When Jack returned his face was dusted with soot. "I secured them all to the fence at the entrance. Smoke is blowing eastward so they'll be okay until rescue arrives."

Adam insisted that Beth take Tess and the dogs next.

Jack agreed. "I'll drive them, bring the cart back and take you, Adam."

Their son nodded.

She smiled shyly at Adam while Tess kissed him goodbye.

"See you in a few minutes," Tess said.

Adam nodded. "I'll be counting down the seconds."

Tess blushed. She and Beth climbed into the cart with Arthur and Poe and Jack sped them to the entrance and out the front gate, which he'd left open. It felt surreal to be on the outside after such strain and struggle. They got off the cart and Jack grinned.

"I'll return with Adam in two shakes," he said.

She smiled as she watched him depart, hardly daring to believe their ordeal might be coming to a close.

They fell into silence as the minutes passed. Beth made sure Tess was wrapped in a blanket as she cuddled Poe. She'd even gotten her to drink some water.

Tess peered out into the darkness. "I see the red lights of the rescuers, but they aren't moving very fast."

"They have to skirt the fires and the vehicles are unwieldy."

Though she should have been too exhausted to move, Beth paced, Arthur following. The smoke was indeed funneling eastward across the park, mingling with the fire that had started kindling behind the venue, then spread to the arcade and now beyond. She saw crowns of orange where the flames had caught the swaying palm trees. As her watch ticked off the minutes, she checked her phone.

One text from Garrett.

OTW.

Help was on the way.

But the danger was still real, as the moments rolled by with no further texts or signs of Adam and Jack.

When she bumped into Arthur after a quick turn, she bent to caress him. He whined low in his throat as if he was wondering the same thing she was.

Where were Jack and Adam?

The smoke thickened, a wall of poison. She handed medical masks from her backpack to Tess. Tess tucked Poe deeper into her jacket. She put masks on Bud and Wyatt, but Daniel shook her off.

The rescuers were still miles away or so it seemed to Beth. Twenty minutes or more had passed since Jack had left to bring Adam out.

Another five minutes and her anxiety ballooned. They should have returned by now.

Had Jack been disoriented? Overcome by the smoke? Had Adam been too heavy for Jack to maneuver into the cart?

Tess was watching her. "Why haven't they come back?"

"I don't know." She checked again to be sure the three prisoners were fully secured before she turned to Tess.

"I need to go look for them." Her phone buzzed with a call. She answered.

"Mom, what is going on? Are you okay? We're five minutes from the park, but stuck behind a slow-moving fire truck."

"I'm okay, but I have to go."

"Go? What...?"

She handed the phone to Tess while Garrett was still firing off questions. When the timbre of the voice changed, she knew the impatient Chase had snatched the phone from him to take over the interrogation.

"It's my family," she told Tess. "Explain what happened. They'll be here shortly to help you."

"Beth." Tess's eyes were enormous with fear.

"Arthur will find them."

Arthur flapped his ears, circling in his excitement as she pulled Jack's hat from her pack and offered it to him. When he'd got the scent she led him to the entrance. She put the special K-9 mask over his muzzle. It would dull his spectacular tracking skills, but she could not let him risk smoke damage to his lungs and the haze was now impenetrable. He would be able to track the scent and she could take it off if need be to have him reestablish the trail. She pulled a mask over her own nose and mouth and stuffed two in her pockets.

"Low, Arthur." The dog scrunched down and she took the end of the leash.

She called out one more time to Tess. "If my family gets here and I'm not back, they'll find us. Stay out. Keep yourselves safe."

Poe waggled his nose at Arthur and let out a mournful howl.

But Beth didn't acknowledge him.

There was only one thing on her mind.

"Find, Arthur."

Please.

FOURTEEN

When Jack finally jerked the cart to a stop and slammed into the office, Adam was ready. Though he was sitting up, clutching the edge of the cot, it was clear he was weak.

"What took you so long?"

"Smoke's bad. Lots of debris falling too."

"As long as you got our ladies to safety."

It tickled Jack to think of Beth as his lady, a privilege he'd not fully appreciated when it had been true so many decades before. Likely it was a pretense he could enjoy only for a few more hours.

A boom shook the ground, the glow through the office window momentarily backlighting the smoky sky.

"Place is going up one ride at a time," Jack said. "Ready to blow this popsicle stand?"

"More than ready." Adam made it to a standing position with a tug from Jack on his good arm.

"Wrist hurt?"

"Nah," Adam said.

"Lying?"

"Yep," Adam acknowledged.

"We'll be out of here soon." He barely caught Adam as he staggered and almost went down to a knee. "Slow, son."

His own strength was waning too. He was running purely on grit and adrenaline.

After a second try, they made it to the cart and Adam insisted on being propped in the passenger seat. Jack turned the key.

Nothing happened. It took a moment for his dull senses to register panic. "It's got gas. I'll check the engine." Adam gamely hauled himself out and Jack flipped up the seat, reaching into the dark compartment too quickly.

A sharp piece of metal cut through his arm from wrist to elbow.

He jerked back with a grunt, blood flowing warm through his tattered sleeve.

Adam tore a strip from the blanket in the back and wrapped it around Jack's wound as tightly as he was able. The blood immediately started to saturate the makeshift bandage.

"Hurts?" Adam said.

"Nah."

"Lying?"

Jack grinned. "Is this why they say like father like son?"

Adam nodded but their smiles quickly faded.

Jack ignored the searing pain in his arm. "I can't fix this cart. The belt's shredded. Gonna have to walk."

"No," Adam said slowly. "You go. Send the rescuers back for me."

"Not going to happen."

"It's the smartest way."

"Quit talking." Jack shoved his shoulder under Adam's armpit and they began to stagger along toward the front gate.

Sweat mingled with the soot, stinging his forehead. They'd made it several yards before Adam's coughing fit stopped them. Jack felt his son's ribs straining, his body trembling to stay upright. The urgency to deliver him from the poisonous air grew.

"Are you...?"

Jack's question was lost in a rush of movement as a tree, branches flaming, crashed down across their path, sending a wave of hot air whooshing in their faces.

Jack retreated a few staggered steps, and almost released Adam.

"We'll have to circle around the other direction," he shouted over the crackle of burning branches.

Adam might have responded, but he didn't hear. They moved slowly along, step by painful step, until they returned to the office and the dead security cart. An ominous roar began to build as the fire overtook the old wood structures in the park. The window for their escape was closing. Fast.

"New plan," Jack shouted. "We'll try for the tunnel. I'll get the cutters in case Daniel's keys don't work." Even if it was impassable, the air would be cleaner, a cushion until rescuers would hopefully arrive.

Adam understood. The underground exit was their best hope.

With Adam leaning on the cart, Jack hauled out the bolt cutters and hastily tied them onto his back with a computer cord, his grip slick with blood. The smoke had thickened to an impenetrable curtain.

As they set off, Adam's muscles quivered and Jack suspected he was trying not to lean too heavily. It was all Jack could do to keep them both on their feet. Hunched to keep to the cleaner air, they struggled on.

Adam tripped and slid from Jack's grasp.

He landed hard on his stomach.

Jack rolled him over. "Rest a minute."

He needed time too because his strength was flagging,

probably accelerated by the blood leaking from his laceration.

He climbed to his feet and helped his son, his vision going blurry. He realized with a sick flush that he didn't know which direction led to the tunnel. Surrounded by a smothering cloud, he could no longer see the way to the office, the gate, the tunnel. There were no landmarks visible.

His lungs burned and so did his blood. He couldn't let his son down, not now, after a lifetime of wondering, loneliness and prayers that God would allow him to know Adam again. It wasn't possible that it would end this way, here in the smoke, with Beth waiting for him to lead Adam out.

Beth...

He forced himself to his feet. With every last ounce of his strength, he pulled Adam upright. He'd find a way. Somehow.

Beth knew she had to be patient with Arthur. He was hampered by his mask and though she removed it periodically for a quick sniff, the dog was facing an enormous challenge.

He shook his whole body, as if he could fling off the mask, which was protecting his lungs from the horrific smoke.

"You can do it," she said, though she knew he couldn't hear her.

Nose to the ground he led her along an invisible route. The cloud of smoke billowed and roiled until Arthur stopped her.

A massive downed tree blocked the path. Had it blocked the way for the cart? It cost them precious minutes to circumvent the obstacle, but Arthur helped her reorient as they cleared it. At long last, she spotted it.

The cart.

Her heart leapt and they ran.

Arthur circled in confusion at the vehicle. She scanned desperately. Empty. There was no sign of Adam and Jack.

Arthur pawed at a spot on the ground.

She bent close until she noticed the droplets.

Blood.

Her breath caught.

It was blood, no doubt, a puddle of it and then…

A trail leading away from the cart. They followed it to the office. Clearly Jack had gone inside for something and come out again. The sooty ground made it impossible for her to detect the trail. Arthur shook his head again, pawing at the mask. His fur was speckled with ash. She dropped to her knees next to him.

"This is hard. I know. It isn't fair to ask, but can you find them, Arthur? Please? Find."

She allowed him to sniff at the only spot of blood she could see and then she put his mask on again. He darted away around the corner of the office and she followed close. In a matter of moments, she'd become almost completely disoriented as the smoke grabbed her in its tight grip.

The enormity of what she'd risked came home to her.

If Arthur could not find Jack and Adam, they would all die alone, victims of the fire. Even if he could locate them, how would they find a way out? She had no phone, no radio.

All she could do was pray and follow her dog.

Seconds felt like hours as she clutched the leash.

It was growing hard to breathe. Wildly, desperately, she pressed on.

Arthur slowed. Her old dog would be unable to continue soon. What had she done, bringing him into a deathtrap?

With a mighty surge that almost took her off her feet, the dog burst ahead, barking.

Finally she saw a shadow up ahead. She pulled down her mask and shouted. "Jack?"

The shadow moved closer and joy exploded through her.

Jack stopped six feet ahead, swaying on his feet, struggling to hold their son. She ran to them, immediately adding her strength to support the two men.

"Oh, P.," Jack said, his voice pained. "Why'd you come?"

"Are you kidding? Think I was going to leave my men here to die?"

Adam was sagging, barely conscious.

Jack shook his head. "Too dangerous." He coughed hard and she saw the blood dripping from his arm.

"Afraid to share the limelight with a woman, St. James?" She snatched a length of gauze from her pack and wrapped it tightly around his wound before she placed masks over their faces.

Adam groaned. He was struggling to stay on his feet.

Her joy and misery twined together. "That way?" she pointed.

Jack panted, exhaustion in his voice. "I just don't know, P. I'm sorry."

"I don't either," she admitted. "But we'll keep moving."

"Agreed." He smiled at her, a sad smile, filled with pride, affection and something deeper.

He firmed his grip around her and Adam. "Not such a bad family, huh?"

She swallowed a lump in her throat as she pulled Jack and Adam closer. Adam gripped her shoulder. *And they'd finish as a family.*

They made it only a few steps before Adam stumbled and they had to stop.

Frustration fired her nerves. Every second of delay allowed the toxins to infiltrate their lungs. Were they headed the right way? Or deeper into the fire?

She stiffened. "Listen."

Jack cocked his head to the sky. "What is that?"

She strained to hear over her own pounding heart. "It's howling. The bloodhounds. I hear them barking."

Arthur heard them too. He waggled his tail hard and angled his body toward the noise.

"This way," Beth said. "Arthur will follow the sound."

Hope gave them enough strength to continue on, foot after foot as the cacophony climbed to new decibel levels.

The mournful, deafening baying of the Wolfe pack grew louder as they hurried on.

"Come on," she urged, when Adam began to sink.

Jack struggled to prop him up and move forward, but Adam crumpled to the ground.

She knelt to him, face wet with tears. "Please, Adam, just a little farther."

Jack was attempting to hoist him upright when Chase and Garrett raced forward through the smoke.

Beth would have whooped aloud if she wasn't so breathless.

The boys didn't waste a moment on chitchat. Chase draped Adam over his shoulder and Garrett helped Beth support Jack. As they neared the front gate, two firefighters with flashlights rushed up to help.

Once they cleared the fence, her boys carried them to a spot farther away from the smoke where a frantic Tess and Poe were waiting.

Beth sank down, hugging Arthur and removing his mask. "He needs water," she called, but Garrett was already pouring a bowlful that Arthur began to slurp.

Steph, Roman, Kara and their dogs hastened over to join them, until it was a mass of chaos and slobber. Medics followed and began treating Jack and Adam.

"You are in big trouble, Mom," Chase said.

"Later." Steph elbowed him. "The police kept us out at first so we decided maybe the dog chorus might help you find your way if you were lost."

"It did," she said. "We wouldn't have made it otherwise."

"Garrett and Chase decided enough was enough and they went in anyway," Steph said, sponging a wet cloth over her mother's face.

She peered around her daughter. Adam was on a stretcher, Tess beside him, Poe licking his face. Her fear ebbed slightly, more so when she saw Jack waving off the medics who'd managed to get a better bandage on his arm before he plodded over to her.

"You shouldn't be moving around," she said.

"Yes, ma'am." He collapsed on the ground next to her. "Just doing a welfare check on you."

"I'm okay and so is Arthur."

He smiled. "Best news, P. Best ever."

Beth blushed as she realized her five children were clustered around, staring at her. Jack squirmed, silent. It was up to her when and how much she would disclose. He wouldn't force the issue. She cleared her throat.

"Kids," she said. "You know Jack. He was more than a friend. He was my high school sweetheart." She gestured to Adam and took an enormous breath. "And this is our son, Adam."

The children stared at Beth. Jack laced his fingers through hers.

"Uh," he said, "I'm sorry this is how it all came out, but—"

"I'm not," Beth said. "I wouldn't have had the courage if God hadn't worked it out this way."

Chase shook his head. "Mom, you've got some explaining to do." They all looked over to see Poe launch himself atop their new half brother. Chase laughed. "Looks like we're going to increase the pack, aren't we?"

Beth nodded as Jack pulled her close, tears washing the grief away one drop at a time.

Six months to the day from their harrowing escape, Beth stood in the church courtyard, admiring the spring sunshine that glistened off the white satin ribbons and the pink rose centerpieces. After a rugged winter, spring had arrived early, bathing Whisper Valley in green. The perfect setting for a fresh beginning.

Beneath an archway trimmed in roses and hydrangeas, Adam beamed at his new wife as they posed for photos. Tess giggled, cheeks pink with joy. She was elegant in her fit and flare gown, a rhinestone comb holding back her mass of curls.

Fully healed, Adam was broad-shouldered and slim, like Jack, but she thought she could see herself in his smile. It was surreal, all of it. Though Adam and Tess had made sure she and Jack were involved in the wedding planning, it was still incredible to think she'd just witnessed her first-born son married to the love of his life, especially after they'd all come so close to dying.

Adam laughed at something Tess whispered to him. He caught Beth watching him and waved.

She waved back, overwhelmed again at the sweetness of the moment.

Jack moved to her and draped an arm around her shoulders. He was beyond handsome in his suit and tie, the crow's feet enhancing the caramel of his eyes. "Apologies to the bride, but you are the best-looking woman in the room."

Her face went warm in that way that was becoming routine, the more days they spent together. As the police investigation into the Cumberland brothers' crimes concluded, there seemed to be endless additional reasons why Jack needed to visit Whisper Valley. The fishing was the best, he proclaimed. There were a couple of potential summer rentals for planned vacations he'd needed to check out. And then he'd wanted to be there for the consultations with a local veterinarian about the best type of doggie wheelchair for Poe, who would go to live with Adam and Tess after their honeymoon. He'd tagged along while Adam got to know his half siblings. Jack was a fixture in their kitchen and the kids had grown comfortable with his presence.

So had she.

More than comfortable. He'd held her hand while she'd cried during the initial conversations with Adam, processed it all during their walks with Arthur along the river. The talks felt so short but lasted for hours as the ease between them grew into...what?

She was unsure where their relationship was headed, afraid to think about it too much. Instead she contented herself with enjoying the companionship of a man she'd lost and found again, not as a spouse, but as a best friend.

Guests began filling up the space, many of whom were unfamiliar since they were friends of the bride and groom. There were also guests from town she'd known since she was a child, people from church, Tess's parents and Adam's adoptive mother and father.

It had been a painful blessing to get to know both of them, the people who had stepped in to be her son's family when she could not. They were wonderful, faithful people, just the kind she'd prayed her son would be able to call Mom and Dad.

She and Jack wandered to the table where a tall candle flickered inside a hurricane lamp. There were photos to commemorate those who were no longer there. Tess's grandmother and Adam's adopted uncle. She gasped when she saw the photo of her late husband Martin.

Adam had asked her about Martin, eager to learn all he could about Beth and her family, her husband, her children—his half siblings. They'd talked for hours and she'd desperately wished Martin could have been there to meet Adam. She looked at his photo, and thought how very proud he would be of the family they'd made. Six beautiful children... and a whole pack of dogs. Martin would have welcomed Adam with open arms.

Her late husband had never as much as hinted to anyone about her secret. "When you've healed enough, you'll know it and you'll be able to speak your truth."

And she did know it, and she was so deeply grateful to God that He'd kept her in the palm of His hand, even when she hadn't realized it. "Martin would be so pleased, by all of this," she said, around a lump in her throat.

"Wish I could have met him. I know we would have liked each other," Jack said. "We'd go fishing and watch football. We'd have been buddies."

She laughed. "You're right. He'd have you on his bowling team in a flash."

"Exactly. We'd have so much in common, especially the most important thing."

"What's that?"

Jack took her hands and kissed her knuckle. "We both love you."

Her eyes flew wide. "Did you say the *L* word?"

"You know I did, P. It's not a surprise to you, is it? You are the smartest woman I know and you have to have sensed that I'm in deep over you."

She looked away because she had sensed it, both in herself and in him, but she'd not allowed herself to consider what it might mean.

"I want us to get married."

Her pulse thumped. "It hasn't been that long..."

"Uh-uh. Not going to listen to that excuse. We're both grown-ups. We've lived enough to know who we are and what we want." He faced her and tipped her chin up. "I want you."

"I...it's not that simple."

"Yes, it is. It's totally that simple." He pointed. "And they agree."

Standing across the room looking at them were her two daughters and four sons, a son-in-law and four daughters by marriage. Every dog, sitting in a neat row, sported a bow-tie, except for Phil, whom they hadn't even tried to clothe, and Poe, whom Tess had somehow gotten into a little vest. Chase's bloodhound, Tank, had shredded his. The humans were all smiling at her, beaming as a matter of fact.

"You talked to them?"

"Yes, ma'am. We prayed together to be precise. And they all agree that this is right, and God approved." He paused. "And that your husband, Martin, would agree too, because he loved you and wanted the best for you...and so do I. That's why you should marry me."

Her breath hitched but she couldn't speak.

He went on. "We were together in our teens, but not in the right way. I know now the worth of things. The worth of you and me together. It's not enough for me to watch our son's life from the sidelines with you. God's given us a chance to show up. Together. Are you ready for it, P.?"

She took the deepest breath of her life and nodded.

With a broad grin, he gave Steph a thumbs-up. He winked at Beth. "We've been practicing this next part."

Steph offered Arthur a small heart-shaped pillow and he trotted over to Beth and Jack.

"Good dog," Jack said.

Arthur presented Jack with the pillow upon which was tied a delicate gold ring, inset with six small diamonds. One for each of her six children, she realized. The larger stone would be for her and Jack.

He untied it and held it up.

"Not as beautiful as you deserve, but it's a starting point."

The gems sparkled in the light. Was this really happening?

Arthur wagged his tail as if he was trying to convince her she wasn't dreaming.

Jack held out the ring to her, eyes shining. "Beth, I love you. Will you marry me?"

"Yes," she said, certain for the first time in many years. "I will, because I love you too."

Jack kissed her, the baying of the hounds ringing around them.

* * * * *

Dear Reader,

It's bittersweet to finish this book, the last in the Security Hounds series. Over the last six stories, I've really come to know and love the Wolfe family and their shaggy pack of dogs. I especially adore the mixed-breed additions to the bloodhound pack, notably Pudge, Phil and Poe. It's time to move on to another series, now that everyone has gotten their happy endings, but I will miss these characters for sure.

The third book, *Hunted on the Trail*, will always be extra special to me, and not only because Pudge sprang to life within its pages, but because it was my fiftieth book with Harlequin's Love Inspired line. I am still not sure how the time passed so quickly, but it has been an absolute blessing to work with such an amazing company. From the art department, to the editors, and everyone in-between, they are simply the dream team and I am grateful God brought us together.

So thank you, Harlequin, and thank you, dear readers, for coming along on the journey with me. Here's to new stories and lots of great reading ahead!

God bless!

Dana

Get up to 4 Free Books!

We'll send you 2 free books from each series you try
PLUS a free Mystery Gift.

FREE Value Over **$25**

Both the **Love Inspired®** and **Love Inspired® Suspense** series feature compelling novels filled with inspirational romance, faith, forgiveness and hope.

YES! Please send me 2 FREE novels from the Love Inspired or Love Inspired Suspense series and my FREE gift (gift is worth about $10 retail). After receiving them, if I don't wish to receive any more books, I can return the shipping statement marked "cancel." If I don't cancel, I will receive 6 brand-new Love Inspired Larger-Print books or Love Inspired Suspense Larger-Print books every month and be billed just $7.19 each in the U.S. or $7.99 each in Canada. That is a savings of 20% off the cover price. It's quite a bargain! Shipping and handling is just 50¢ per book in the U.S. and $1.25 per book in Canada.* I understand that accepting the 2 free books and gift places me under no obligation to buy anything. I can always return a shipment and cancel at any time by calling the number below. The free books and gift are mine to keep no matter what I decide.

Choose one: ☐ **Love Inspired Larger-Print** (122/322 BPA G36Y) ☐ **Love Inspired Suspense Larger-Print** (107/307 BPA G36Y) ☐ **Or Try Both!** (122/322 & 107/307 BPA G36Z)

Name (please print)

Address   Apt. #

City   State/Province   Zip/Postal Code

Email: Please check this box ☐ if you would like to receive newsletters and promotional emails from Harlequin Enterprises ULC and its affiliates. You can unsubscribe anytime.

Mail to the **Harlequin Reader Service:**
IN U.S.A.: P.O. Box 1341, Buffalo, NY 14240-8531
IN CANADA: P.O. Box 603, Fort Erie, Ontario L2A 5X3

Want to explore our other series or interested in ebooks? Visit www.ReaderService.com or call 1-800-873-8635.

---

*Terms and prices subject to change without notice. Prices do not include sales taxes, which will be charged (if applicable) based on your state or country of residence. Canadian residents will be charged applicable taxes. Offer not valid in Quebec. This offer is limited to one order per household. Books received may not be as shown. Not valid for current subscribers to the Love Inspired or Love Inspired Suspense series. All orders subject to approval. Credit or debit balances in a customer's account(s) may be offset by any other outstanding balance owed by or to the customer. Please allow 4 to 6 weeks for delivery. Offer available while quantities last.

Your Privacy—Your information is being collected by Harlequin Enterprises ULC, operating as Harlequin Reader Service. For a complete summary of the information we collect, how we use this information and to whom it is disclosed, please visit our privacy notice located at https://corporate.harlequin.com/privacy-notice. Notice to California Residents – Under California law, you have specific rights to control and access your data. For more information on these rights and how to exercise them, visit https://corporate.harlequin.com/california-privacy. For additional information for residents of other U.S. states that provide their residents with certain rights with respect to personal data, visit https://corporate.harlequin.com/other-state-residents-privacy-rights/.

LIRLIS25